NIGHT CRY

Kendell Paine, a returned war hero, gets into a fight with another gambler, who is later knifed at their gambling club. It looks like Paine might be the guilty party. It's Lt. Mark Deglin's job to track him down. But Paine is in no mood for the third degree, and Deglin ends up accidentally beating him to death. Deglin knows he will never be considered for promotion with a killing on his record—accidental or not—so he sets out to cover it up.

But Deglin doesn't figure on Paine's girl, Morgan, who is waiting for Paine to come back. She and Paine had argued that night but nothing so serious that he would completely disappear. And there's Smith, the journalist who just won't let the story go, and allies himself with Morgan. Now Captain Knight has put Deglin in charge of tracking down the missing man. As carefully as Deglin keeps covering his tracks, it all slowly begins to unravel.

"Excellently planned, tense and hard-bitten."
—*New Yorker*

"If you like noir, just read it… Things get complicated and dark." —*Olman's Fifty*

William L. Stuart Bibliography

Novels:
The Dead Lie Still (1945)
Night Cry (1948)
Dead Ahead (1953)

TV Scripts / Story:
NBC Presents (1949)
Colgate Theatre (1949)
The Accused (1953)
Man Against Crime (1952-53)
Crime Syndicate (1952-53)
Pentagon U.S.A. (1953)
Danger (1953)
Martin Kane (1954)
Mark Stevens in Big Town (1955)
The Man Called X (1956)
Lux Video Theatre (1957)
Matinee Theatre (1957)
Zane Grey Theatre (1958)
Richard Diamond, Private Detective (1958)
Kraft Theatre (1958)
Perry Mason (1959)
77 Sunset Strip (1958-59)
Sugarfoot (1960)
Bourbon Street Beat (1960)
Surfside 6 (1960)
Hawaiian Eye (1961)
Bronco (1961)
Rawhide (1962)
The Gallant Men (1963)
Bonanza (1963-65)
Days of Our Lives (1966)
Daniel Boone (1966)
The Green Hornet (1966-67)
Land of the Giants (1969-70)
You Lie So Deep, My Love (TV Movie; 1975)

NIGHT CRY

WILLIAM L. STUART

Introduction by Curtis Evans

Stark House Press • Eureka California

NIGHT CRY

Published by Stark House Press
1315 H Street
Eureka, CA 95501, USA
griffinskye3@sbcglobal.net
www.starkhousepress.com

NIGHT CRY
Originally published by The Dial Press, Inc., New York, and copyright ©
1948 by William L. Stuart. Reprinted in paperback by Avon Books, New
York, 1949.

Reprinted by permission of the agent on behalf of the William L. Stuart
estate. All rights reserved under International and Pan-American
Copyright Conventions.

"Blue Knight's Gambit" © 2025 by Curtis Evans

ISBN: 979-8-88601-153-1

Cover & Text design by Mark Shepard, shepgraphics.com
Proofreading by Bill Kelly

PUBLISHER'S NOTE:
This is a work of fiction. Names, characters, places and incidents are
either the products of the author's imagination or used fictionally, and
any resemblance to actual persons, living or dead, events or locales, is
entirely coincidental.
Without limiting the rights under copyright reserved above, no part of
this publication may be reproduced, stored, or introduced into a retrieval
system or transmitted in any form or by any means (electronic,
mechanical, photocopying, recording or otherwise) without the prior
written permission of both the copyright owner and the above publisher
of the book.

First Stark House Press Edition: May 2025

7
Blue Knight's Gambit
by Curtis Evans

17
Night Cry
by William L. Stuart

Blue Knight's Gambit

William L. Stuart's *Night Cry* (1948)

By Curtis Evans

"What do you think, Mark?" Smith asked.
"I just work here," Deglin said.
"I know," Smith said, nodding.
"It's just the goddam racket we're in."

In 1949 in the case of *Wolf v. Colorado*, the United States Supreme Court declined generally to apply to individual states the federal exclusionary rule, established thirty-five years earlier in the case of *Boyd v. United States*, that evidence obtained by federal law enforcement officers in violation of the Fourth Amendment of the Constitution (*the people's right to be secure in their persons, houses, papers and effects, against unreasonable searches and seizures, shall not be violated....*) must be excluded from evidence. While seventeen states had adopted the federal exclusionary rule by 1949, thirty states had explicitly rejected it. For the next dozen years the Supreme Court applied the exclusionary rule to states only in cases where police had obtained evidence through coercion, violence or brutality shocking to the conscience. For example, the Court in 1952 ruled that, in a case where California police had had a man strapped to a hospital operating table, a tube forced into his throat and stomach and fed an emetic solution in order to cause him to vomit two morphia tablets he had swallowed when the officers had burst into his room without a search warrant, the tablets (or what remained of them) must be excluded from evidence. It was not until 1961 in the landmark case of *Mapp v. Ohio* that the Supreme Court finally ruled that the exclusionary rule applied to states as well as the federal government, meaning that throughout the decade of the 1950s the Court was in the devilish business of subjectively determining when state police had "shocked the conscience."

Whatever judges might have thought of various police searches in the law racket back in that day it is fair to say that the performance of ace lawman Mark Deglin in William L. Stuart's 1948 superb crime novel *Night Cry* is about as shocking to the conscience as police behavior can get. In the novel devilishly handsome Lieutenant Deglin, lauded in the admiring press as the police force's "Mister Tough," quickly proves himself no "blue knight" as it were, but rather a wolf in plain clothing. During the course of his investigation of the fatal stabbing of a man at a gambling key club, Deglin savagely beats to death a resisting suspect, whom he soon afterwards learns is entirely innocent of the crime. Seemingly he feels little if any remorse over Kendall Paine, the surly "punk" he just killed, impassively reflecting "this was the first person he had killed himself. He'd beaten many men and a couple of women. But this was the first dead one." Indeed, Deglin's instant impulse, which he soon resourcefully puts into effect, is to cover up his crime by making the dead man disappear.

What follows next is a uniquely interesting fusion of a classic Croftsian alibi plot (there is even mention of a timetable) with Woolrichian noirish atmospherics. This tarnished blue knight devises a clever gambit to escape capture, but gradually the maneuver starts to come undone in the manner of best-laid plans, in the process implicating innocent people like Ken Paine's lovely, long-suffering society girlfriend Morgan Taylor. Will Deglin's slumbering conscience awaken? And if so, just what will he do then?

One of the striking aspects of this tautly suspenseful crime tale is the author's uncompromising refusal to give his presumably largely pro-cop late forties readership a break when it comes to sympathizing with Deglin, at least at the beginning of the story. At a time when thousands upon thousands of American crime fiction readers were cheering on Mickey Spillane's repulsive psychotic dick Mike Hammer sadistically slaughtering subversive Commies and transgressive women with his own bare hands, William L. Stuart declined to provide an easy moral out for his own novel's murderous protagonist. On behalf of the cops' Mr. Tough, he provides little in the way of exculpatory evidence. Ken Paine is sullen and

BLUE KNIGHT'S GAMBIT

self-destructive, to be sure, but he, unlike Deglin, is no murderer in the story which Stuart unfolds. Rather Ken is an "All-American Boy" sadly run to seed, a college football and world war hero obviously suffering from some form of PTSD, if this exchange between the two men in any indication:

> "Did you knife those Japs," Deglin said.
> Paine rubbed his neck. What Japs?"
> "All those Japs you killed."
> "They weren't Japs. They were Krauts."
> "Did you knife them, too?"
> "I knifed them, and I choked them and—what the hell are you talking about?"

In mitigation of his murder we learn that Deglin is bitter about having been passed over for a desired promotion. It is not enough, in my view, nor do I think the author himself thought so:

> "Doc, you know I'm one of the best detectives on the force and you know they shouldn't have passed over me. I was as eligible as Knight. Captain Knight. Jesus!"
> "Acting captain," the doctor said.
> "Acting crap," Deglin said.

Some reviewers of Stuart's crime novel were, shall we say, a teensy bit *euphemistic* in their discussions of Deglin's criminal transgression. The notice in the Oklahoma City *Daily Oklahoman* states that "Wegin [sic]…hits [Paine] a little too hard," while the reviewer for the Louisville *Courier-Journal* declares that the lawman "manhandles a belligerent suspect a shade too vigorously." I shall leave it for the reader to decide for him/herself how these descriptions comport with the crime as the author actually portrays it.

Where virtually all reviewers were agreed, however, was in their assessments that the book made one terrific read. In the *Chicago Tribune* Drexel Drake pronounced that *Night Cry* "bores into the vitals." Dorothy B. Hughes deemed it "an honest, exciting and curiously haunting story" with "a fine plot, handled without flaw and with overwhelming suspense." Miriam Ottenberg selected it as one of the best crime yarns of the year, with "the year's most unforgettable criminal." The most memorable take on the novel, however, came from David Ormont at the *Brooklyn Eagle*, who wrote:

> Mr. Stuart knows the underworld characters and their argot. He is well-versed in the intricacies of the police court. He can spin a yarn with the best of them. His style is terse and breezy and there is no letting up in interest from the beginning to the very end. His characters are not mere puppets; he infuses them with life and breath.
>
> .... Mr. Stuart bears watching as a clever writer of this genre of tale. Dashiell Hammett and Rex Stout had better look to their laurels!

That last line unsurprisingly was blurbed by Avon when the reprint publisher issued the novel in paperback the next year. Avon reprinted *Night Cry* two more times over the next few years and additionally the novel was adapted as a lauded 1950 crime film under the title *Where the Sidewalk Ends*. The film, which was helmed by *Laura* director Otto Preminger, reunited *Laura* lovebirds Dana Andrews and Gene Tierney in a far grittier and less glamorous film, though one which repeatedly pulls the novel's hard punches. While *Night Cry* can legitimately be described as a noir novel, the film, in my opinion, though certainly a well-crafted and entertaining melodrama, is too light for true noir.

Critically Ben Hecht's screenplay for *Sidewalk* makes Dana Andrews' Mark Deglin, renamed Mark Dixon in the film, far more sympathetic than the character in the novel. Ken Paine, Dixon's supposed victim, becomes a nasty gambler's tout, employed by a hoodlum named Tommy Scalise (Gary Merrill), an amalgam of two minor characters from the novel (one of whom remains only a name in the book, never actually appearing). At a hotel gambling party Paine viciously slaps Morgan Taylor (Gene Tierney), his estranged wife in the film, and later at his apartment he violently attacks Dixon with a liquor bottle, so that Dixon's blows on Paine clearly constitute self-defense, making Dixon's subsequent attempt to cover-up Paine's death simply look foolish. Worse, the film has Karl Malden's by-the-books Lieutenant Thomas, another invented character, crucially decide suddenly to beat information out of a man in order to get the goods on Scalise, which undermines the anti-police brutality message of the novel.

There are other changes from the book as well, all of which serve to transform a superb noir novel into a mainstream romantic crime melodrama. For example, glamorous Gene Tierney, transformed into a runway model in the film—her then husband, fashion designer Oleg Cassini, even makes a cameo appearance as himself—and improbably given a lovable, school-of-hard-knocks taxi driver father, becomes Mark Dixon's straight-out love interest, with his actual ambiguous love interest from the book, torch singer Jane Corby, ruthlessly expunged by Hecht.

On the plus side, Gary Merrill delivers a terrific performance as nattily dressed, Benzedrine inhaling, silkily sinister Tommy Scalise. (1950 was arguably the peak point of Merrill's acting career, with this and his co-starring role in the Oscar-winning *All About Eve*.) Sneeringly derided with the handle "Dream Boy" by Dixon and surrounding himself with a bevy of male musclemen to do his wicked bidding (most notably Neville Brand's buff bruiser Steve), the character has "strong gay connotations," Preminger biographer Chris Fujiwara has noted. Also notable in this context is the intense devotion which Dixon's cop colleague Detective Paul Klein (Bert Freed) displays for his buddy. Klein passionately tells Dixon, albeit to no avail, not to let himself be led astray by Tierney's pretty face but later begs his wife to let him lend Dixon three hundred dollars (about $3800 today), screwing up his face in utter anguish when he thinks she will refuse. This is all interesting stuff indeed, but none of it comes from the novel. Like Mark Devlin himself, *Night Cry* hits hard, much harder than the film, giving noir fans a 100-proof slug of the genuine article.

Eight years later in 1958 Hollywood took a second crack at *Night Cry* when it was adapted for the acclaimed live television anthology series *Kraft Theatre*, this time under its original title and apparently much more faithfully. This adaptation starred Jack Klugman as Mark Deglin (same name as the book this time) and featured, for all of a five-minute scene, then virtually unknown, thirty-year-old actor Peter Falk as dangerously imperiled police informant "Izzy," another character from the book who had been deleted from the 1950 film. According to the episode scripter, the late Larry Cohen, who was then all of twenty-two (this was his second filmed script), Falk during his short screen time completely stole the show from Klugman, drawing a great deal of favorable attention in the business and effectively launching his long film and television career. Oscar-nominated supporting roles in 1960 and 1961 films soon followed for the beloved actor, along with a lengthy leading turn on television as a certain cop named Columbo, a role which would net Falk three Emmy Awards in the 1970s. Ironically Lieutenant Columbo had been originated a decade earlier by rumpled *Sidewalk* supporting actor Bert Freed, who in 1960 played the astute police detective on an episode of *The Chevy Mystery Show*.

■ ■ ■

William Lisle Stuart, the author of *Night Cry*, was born in the little town of Princeton, Missouri on March 13, 1912. His father, James Lisle Stuart, was a railroad telegraph operator and the family moved around the Plains rather a bit in Bill's youth, finally settling during the Roaring Twenties in the rather more happening metropolis of Chicago. In 1930 Bill graduated from the all-male Crane Tech High School, where he was a feature writer and cartoonist on the school newspaper. A smart and strappingly handsome, blonde-haired, blue-eyed youth who stood at 5' 10" and weighed 160 pounds, Bill at the height of the Depression found work in the newspapers, within a few years becoming a nationally syndicated columnist as *Screen & Radio Weekly*'s Radio Reporter.

In 1933 Bill at the age of twenty wed Dorothy Ann Badger, daughter of a Chicago stockbroker and Board of Trade member. Dorothy was five years older than Bill, a divorcee with a five-year-old son. The couple remained together until her death in 1962, together having two daughters, Ann and Shelley, during the Forties. By this time Bill and Dorothy had moved to New York City, where they lived in a swanky apartment in Manhattan (today the Renwick

Hotel). Bill worked as a publicist with the advertising firm of Young and Rubicam, making $5000 a year or about $110,000 today, while Dorothy was employed as a secretary in the same firm. (Their top client was Jell-O.) By 1950 the family had moved forty miles out of NYC to the pleasant, affluent suburban city of Ramapo, but they were soon to make a much longer trek.

Like several other clever mid-century admen, such as Alan Green and Henry Slesar (both of them first novel Edgar Award winners), Bill Stuart decided to try his hand at crime writing, publishing *The Dead Lie Still*, an espionage thriller, in 1945 and *Night Cry* three years later. Reviewers lavished praise on both novels, but after the success of *Where the Sidewalk Ends* Bill dropped out of the novel business and with his family moved across the coast to California to work in the burgeoning television industry. In 1960 the family was living several hours out of LA in an attractive Prairie-style house in the town of Corcoran. During the Fifties and Sixties Bill was a prolific TV series writer, turning out scripts for such crime and mystery programs as *Man Against Crime*, *Crime Syndicate*, *Danger*, *The Man Called X*, *Richard Diamond, Private Detective*, and, last but certainly not least, *Perry Mason* ("The Case of the Jaded Joker"). Bill also wrote for westerns, including *Bonanza*, and he produced the fifth and final season of *Maverick*. His final writing credit was in 1975 for the ABC Movie of the Week *You Lie So Deep, My Love*, a tense domestic suspense thriller starring *Ironside* alumni Don Galloway and Barbara Anderson. Thirteen years later William L. Stuart died in Los Angeles at the age of seventy-five on January 11, 1988, forty years after publishing *Night Cry*, first editions of which are now valuable collector's items. Nearly another forty years after the author's death, this classic crime novel happily is finally back in print once again.

—February 2025

Curtis Evans received a PhD in American history in 1998. He is the author of *Masters of the "Humdrum" Mystery: Cecil John Charles Street, Freeman Wills Crofts, Alfred Walter Stewart and British Detective Fiction, 1920-1961* (2012), *Clues and Corpses: The Detective Fiction and Mystery Criticism of Todd Downing* (2013), *The Spectrum of English Murder: The Detective Fiction of Henry Lancelot Aubrey-Fletcher and G. D. H. and Margaret Cole* (2015) and editor of the Edgar nominated *Murder in the Closet: Essays on Queer Clues in Crime Fiction Before Stonewall* (2017). He writes about vintage crime fiction at his blog The Passing Tramp and at Crimereads.

NIGHT CRY

WILLIAM L. STUART

This book
is for
Big A and
little a

1

It could have been a party, polite and well-bred. The room was long, softly lighted. A cannel-coal fire burned cheerfully on the grate. Most of the guests were in evening dress, and their conversation was only a soft murmur enclosed by the richly-paneled walls. Two white-coated servants moved discreetly about, silver trays laden. The guests nodded and removed the glasses and replaced them.

It could have been a polite, well-bred party in the brownstone mansion, excepting for naked greed in the eyes of some, intentness in the eyes of others, the faintest of undercurrents of despair and hope—and the clicking of dice, the rattle of the tiny ivory ball in the wheel, and the soft monotonous voices of the croupier and the house man.

At the dice game, only the girl was not looking down into the long, high-walled, felt-lined table. The dice rolled across the marked and lettered surface and hit the rail and spun for a moment. The house man's rake moved swiftly, pulling in the brown and blue and red chips, rearranging the patterns in front of the players. The dice went across the table and the voice said, softly, without emotion, "Coming out."

"Ken," the girl said.

He tore his eyes from the green cloth and turned to her.

"Yes." His voice was fogged with impatience.

"Don't you think we'd better go, Ken?" she asked.

His eyes returned hungrily to the dice which spun and stopped.

"You made me miss that one," he said, without looking at her. "I was going to play it for a crap and he crapped."

"I'm sorry," she said contritely. She was a lovely girl with dark hair and a slim, straight figure. Her face paled and her grey eyes were luminous and large in her face. She kept her eyes on his handsome, intent profile but she said nothing more as the dice moved around the table. He played now and again, grimacing when

NIGHT CRY 19

it went against him. When one of the waiters went by, he took two of the brandies, drank one and handed the glass back and held the other, his attention still on the play.

The dice came to him and he drank the second brandy. He put the glass down and picked up the dice. He held them in his hands, nursing them, looking down at the small pile of chips in front of him inside the rail.

"Coming out," the house man said, an edge to the softness.

Ken's eyes lifted and glittered at the man. "Take your time," he snapped.

He looked down at the chips and then pushed them all out. The cubes moved in his hands, then he leaned over the box and rolled them. The rake snaked out and stopped them.

"Against the wall," the voice said softly.

He took the dice again and she could feel his arm tremble under the rough tweed of his sports jacket.

"Please, Ken," she said.

He flung the dice and they hit and rolled wildly, spinning.

"Point four," the house man said. He flicked them back across the cloth to Ken, and Ken held them for an instant. Then he threw again.

"Seven," the house man said, and the rake moved the cubes along the table.

The young man took the girl by the arm hard and they stepped back. "Let's get a drink, Morgan," he said.

They moved across the room, past the roulette wheel and its ring of seated players, to a sideboard. He poured brandy into two tall glasses.

"Morgan," he said. His eyes had a flame in them.

"Yes?"

"Got any money?"

"A little. But I should get home, Ken. Really."

"What's the matter?" He looked down at her and the flame grew. "Getting a little tired of a maladjusted person?"

"It isn't that, Ken. You—you shouldn't be gambling and you shouldn't be—" She stopped, but her eyes went to the glass in his hand.

"You're like all the rest," he said thinly. He finished the glass, and coughed once. "Let me have twenty," he said.

She hesitated, then she opened her handbag and handed him a twenty-dollar bill. He nodded and went to a desk. A moment later, he returned with four brown chips. "Come on," he said.

She followed him back to the table. The players were as they had been before, intent on the play, listening to the drone of the house man, excepting that where Ken had stood, a heavily built man was playing. His eyes were deep-set in folds of pink, massaged flesh. He had been drinking but his hands manipulated a stack of chips with easy dexterity.

The young man tapped him on the shoulder and the older turned his head slowly. He looked but he didn't say anything. Then he turned back to the play.

"You've got my place," Ken said, his words trembling.

"Now it's my place," the big man said without turning.

"I went to get more chips."

The big man looked across at the house man. "Charlie," he said.

Charlie looked up from the play, his eyes impersonal.

"You've developed an annoying clientele, Charlie," the big man said.

The voices stopped. The movement of the dice stopped.

Tension spread through the room slowly, like oil, and a tall dark man moved softly across from the roulette table.

Ken moved. He pulled on the big man's shoulder. The big man came from the table fast. He hit Ken heavily in the face and the young man sprawled back, grabbing for support. He fell slowly, carrying a lamp off a table, and as he fell he watched the big man intently. He got to one knee and shook his head as the big man laughed shortly and moved toward him again. Then Ken came suddenly to his feet, a heavy ashtray in his hand. He swung and the big man turned and fell. The ashtray hit the rug and rolled.

Then the tall dark man was in front of him.

"All right, Paine," he said. "Get out."

"I'll kill him," Ken said. His voice trembled.

"Get out," the tall man said again. He turned to the house man. "Charlie," he said. "Get him out of here. I'll take care of Morrison."

He stood beside the fallen man, doing nothing about him, watching as the young man and the girl moved across the room. Then he

NIGHT CRY

leaned over and said flatly, "Come on. You're okay."

The big man got carefully to his feet, swaying slightly, as though he were suddenly feeling the effects of the liquor. Blood moved slowly down one cheek. They left the room together, the big man and the tall one.

For the space of a moment there was silence. Then someone laughed, and the quiet voices began again. The roulette wheel spun and the ball made its light clatter. When the tall man returned some minutes later, the room was much as it had been before.

He moved around the room, his dark eyes nervous and alert, his long white hands working. He looked quickly from face to face, checking each expression—the intensity of the players, the easy watchfulness of the house men.

As he started toward a rear door opposite that leading into the foyer, the woman screamed—softly at first, then piercingly. He turned quickly on the balls of his feet.

The woman screamed again at the door to the foyer.

Deglin, kneeling beside the body, lifted his head as the door opened. The muscle twitched in the side of his jaw and he rubbed it automatically. The young cop who stuck his head in the door said, "It's Smith, Lieutenant," and Deglin got to his feet. He went to the door and pulled it the rest of the way open. The light from the entryway in back of him cast a warm radiance into the night and caught Smith's worn, bored face.

"Hello, Clem," Deglin said, without moving.

Smith looked at the broad young cop and at Deglin. Then he grinned slightly. "Okay," he said. "I saw this on the teletype and heard you were up here. I thought I'd see what's doing."

"We don't know yet," Deglin said. "Klein and I just got here."

Smith turned and surveyed the line of cars at the curb.

"Who's here from Homicide?" he said negligently.

"Riley."

"Oh," Smith said. "What about it?"

"We haven't talked to anyone. Go for a stroll."

Smith grinned again. "It's raining," he said.

Deglin shrugged. "The officer here is out. It's raining on him too. It's raining on a hell of a lot of people."

"He was sitting in your cruise car," Smith said.

"Sit in the cruise car then," Deglin said. He closed the door as Smith said thanks. He returned to the body and knelt beside it again. "That was Smith, the West Side man from the *Globe*," he said to Riley; then he added, with some irritation, looking at the body, "I wish we could turn him over."

Riley nodded, but he said nothing. He stood patiently, his hands deep in the pockets of his shining raincoat, and watched the police photographer adjust a gadget on the front of his camera. Klein, the other district detective, had a fold of yellow paper in his hand and was stretching carefully, looking at the foyer, at the body, at the furnishings.

Deglin came to his feet again. He went through the door that led through the small foyer, into the gambling room. There had been some quiet talk but it stopped instantly. Deglin looked without particular interest at the men and women seated in a line against a wall, though they stared at him. Two patrolmen stood near windows, watching. Another was at a chuck-a-luck cage, revolving it idly, so that the dice fell with a subdued clatter.

"Hey, you," Deglin said to him.

The patrolman looked back over his shoulder, then stepped suddenly away.

"Got their names and addresses?" Deglin said.

"Not yet."

"Get at it."

Deglin half sat against the roulette table and watched the patrolman move over to an elderly lady. She looked at him with disdain and said nothing.

"Look, mother," Deglin said, his easy voice carrying across the room, "this is a murder rap. You might as well spring here as at the station."

She glanced at Deglin and said something to the patrolman quite softly. He leaned forward and she said it again and he wrote it down. Then he moved to the next. Deglin lit a cigarette and watched him.

He looked, leaning against the table, much like he always looked. One wouldn't have thought he was a detective. He was, though. One would have thought that he was in some unusual business,

NIGHT CRY

and coldly competent at it. He was that. And one would have thought that he had a look of coolness and bitterness and cruelty about him. Deglin was all those. He sat against the table, appearing no less handsome and competent and hard than he intended to appear. He wore a belted raincoat that showed the spattering of wind-driven rain he had walked through from the police car to the brownstone. His hair and eyes were black and his skin was dark.

A sudden flash of white in the foyer was repeated almost at once. Deglin stood and went back. Riley had already turned the body over, and he and Klein and Deglin looked down upon the man. He was a large man, heavy and grey haired, and he looked quarrelsome and dissolute even in death.

"Nicest thing that could have happened to him," Deglin said. "Think of the hangover he'd have had tomorrow."

Riley grunted. He turned to a heavy man who had been looking at the body. "Isn't much you can do about this one, is there, doc?" he asked.

"Not much," the doctor said. "The knife probably cut the heart in half."

Deglin got down on his knees again.

"Would he have done this in the fall, doc?" he said.

The doctor got down on his knees with a grunt. Deglin pointed to a bruise below the pouched eye.

"How long ago did this happen," the doctor said. "The sticking."

"Half-hour, Jim?" Deglin asked.

Klein nodded.

"More or less," Deglin said to the doctor.

The doctor studied for a bit. "Don't know," he said. "Can't know everything, damn it. Doesn't seem as though there would have been time enough for all this discoloration if he'd gotten this when he was knifed. Heart stopped. Guesswork, of course."

"Maybe he was slugged some time before?" Deglin said.

"Maybe."

Deglin indicated the dead man's left hand. "Look at that."

"Huh," the doctor said. "He hit someone?"

"You tell me," Deglin said.

The doctor was silent. He looked and rubbed the back of his head. "This isn't official, Mark," he said, after a minute.

"Yeah," Deglin said.

"He hit someone hard. He hit him around the same time he was whacked in the eye. I don't think he was hit with a fist. Look."

The detectives looked.

"See under the eye here? Not a very wide bruise. Only one bruise. But there is also a thin, deep cut. It bled. But it's been cleaned up."

"We'll get a blood trace in the can," Deglin said.

"In the wash stand," the doctor said. "I think so."

"Thanks," said Deglin, and got up. The doctor got up, too "Any prints on the knife?" he asked.

Deglin looked at him pityingly.

"Okay," the doctor said. "They can take this guy out of here."

They went to the door together, and on out to the narrow stone porch. The rain came sideways in the wind, and they turned against it. Out on the Hudson, beyond the murky strip of wind-whipped trees along the Drive, the water gleamed dully. A whistle sounded mournfully, caricatured by the wind.

"Thanks, doc," Deglin said. "We'll tear them apart with this in there. They're all ready with the no-seeum no-hearum routine. I can watch them practice shaking their heads."

"Good boy, Mark," the doctor said. He hesitated, and looked off at the river. "Say," he began as though he had just thought of it.

Deglin stiffened and waited.

"I was sorry to hear about the—" the doctor left it unfinished. He glanced at Deglin quickly and turned his face to the river again.

"Things happen," Deglin said.

The doctor shrugged, lighter now that he had said what he had hated having to say. "Oh, well," he said. "Knight's older and he has a lot of responsibilities."

"He's a clown," Deglin said tightly. "He'll have it loused up in a week."

The doctor stood awkwardly for a moment and Deglin let him stand there, knowing he was feeling uncomfortable. Then he said softly, "Doc, you know I'm one of the best detectives on the force and you know they shouldn't have passed over me. I was as eligible as Knight. Captain Knight. Jesus!"

"Acting captain," the doctor said.

"Acting crap," Deglin said.

NIGHT CRY 25

The doctor hesitated for an instant, as though there were something else he might say. Then he shrugged and went heavily down the steps. Deglin watched him get into a battered coupe parked at the head of the line of cars. As the starter ground loudly and the motor of the coupe caught, the door of the cruise car opened and Smith twisted his long legs out. He came up the steps to Deglin.

"How about it now, Mark?"

"Knifing," Deglin said.

Smith stepped into the slight protection of the doorway and Deglin stepped back with him. "Doesn't look like the kind of a joint that would have knifings," Smith observed. "Should be something more high-toned, like a good poisoning."

"It's a gambling joint," Deglin said.

"Oh." Smith laughed shortly. "That cop out in the car has been talking my arm off, but he didn't get around to telling me that."

"Good for him," Deglin said.

Smith looked at him in the darkness. "What in the hell wrong with you, Mark?" he said.

"Not a goddamn thing," Deglin said sharply.

"Okay. Okay," Smith said. "Now, can I come on in the joint or do I have to sit out there and listen to some more of this boy scout's chatter. I'll cover the rest of the boys."

Deglin considered for a moment. "You can come in," he said finally. "But go into the game room and sit down."

"Thanks," Smith said.

Deglin led the way back into the foyer and Smith paused to look at the body. He glanced at Deglin, started to say something, thought better of it, and walked on into the gambling room.

There was a lab man at work in the guest lavatory—Deglin could see him through the partly opened door—and Riley was standing beside Klein, looking at a list of names. Deglin looked over Klein's shoulder.

"Any of them look as though they'd been in a scrap?" he asked as he read.

"Naw," Klein said quickly.

Deglin scowled. "Then whoever the stiff had whacked must have cleared out. Who runs the layout?"

"The tall, shiny looking guy," Klein said. "He was making a move to leave when the patrolman heard the woman screaming. He ain't happy about having to stay around."

Deglin nodded. "We'll talk to him, Dan?" he said to Riley.

Riley nodded, and Klein went into the gambling room.

Deglin got four chairs, one from the gambling room itself, and arranged them in a little square. Riley sat on one and stretched his long legs out and pushed his hat back on his head. Deglin stood until Klein brought in the tall, immaculately dressed man. His eyes looked as though he were a little ill, but he was managing to smile slightly.

"Good evening," he said.

Deglin said hello and pointed to a chair. "Get some of the details out of the way before we go over to the station house," he said.

"While they're still fresh," Riley added.

The tall man nodded and sat down. Deglin sat down and leaned back.

"Okay," he said.

The tall man shrugged.

Deglin looked at Riley and shook his head. Then he looked back again.

"This is your murder, bud," he said. "We don't know a thing about it. What was the guy's name? Was he a regular? Who cut him? Who are your partners? What's your name? Get going."

"This gentleman took my name."

"I know he took it," Deglin said. "I want to see if you can remember it. What is it?"

"Carlstrom," the man said.

"You look like an Italian," Deglin said equably. "But go on."

"The man here has been coming in every now and then. Big player. Big spender."

"Big troublemaker," Riley said easily.

Carlstrom shrugged. "Tonight he had been at the crap table. His luck was good. A half-hour or so ago—maybe longer—he passed the dice and wandered away from the table. A little while later a new party in the doorway screamed. A patrolman had been passing and heard it. When I got to the door, he was already there. We saw the body at the same time."

NIGHT CRY

Deglin nodded. "The patrolman thinks you were going to go right by the body—and keep going."

"Oh, no."

"Who was this new party? Still here?"

"Yes," Carlstrom said. "The old dame."

"Your knife?" Deglin asked.

"Oh, no."

"Understand this is a key place," Deglin said. "Exclusive place for the barracuda."

Carlstrom shrugged.

"What's the guy's name?"

"Morrison. L. O. Morrison."

"Oh, yeah," Deglin said. He looked at the floor. "So that's him."

Carlstrom smiled charmingly. "That was him."

"Yeah," Deglin said. "Who'd he fight with? You?"

"Fight?"

"Don't be simple. We know he had a fight. We know that it wasn't any of your customers who are in there now. Who was it?"

Carlstrom frowned. "I—"

Riley laughed, looking at him. Carlstrom hesitated another minute, then leaned forward in his chair toward Deglin. "I don't like this," he said.

"Oh, sure," Deglin said.

"Really. But Mr. Morrison did mix it up for a minute with a young fellow named Paine. Kendall Paine."

"How much did they mix it up?" Deglin said.

"Quite a bit."

"How long ago?"

"Oh, an hour or so."

Deglin looked at his watch. "About ten-thirty?"

Carlstrom shrugged.

"Tell us about it."

"Well, you see, Lieutenant—" he lifted an eyebrow politely, and when Deglin just looked at him, went on more quickly: "You see, this punk had been drinking heavily and making a lot of trouble."

"What other trouble," Deglin said.

"Well, he'd been arguing with his dame."

Deglin looked at Riley and Klein. Riley shook his head. He got up and walked around his chair, then he sat down. "Look," he said patiently, "will you start at the beginning and tell us what went on? We haven't all night."

"I'm nervous," Carlstrom said.

"All right, shake it out, but get it out someway."

Carlstrom looked at his hands. "You see," he said, and his voice trembled slightly, "you see, this Kendall Paine had come in earlier with a girl. He called her Morgan."

"That's a hell of a name," Deglin said.

Carlstrom licked his lips. "He called her Morgan," he said. "He got pretty drunk and they had some arguments. She wanted him to leave. He was tough with everybody—argued with the dealers—and the other customers."

"Why didn't you throw him out?"

"We did. After he had the trouble with Morrison."

"He was a pretty mean character, eh?" Deglin said. "Drunk and nasty. Do you think he could have killed Morrison?"

Carlstrom shrugged.

"You know," Deglin said. "You throw him out, and he thinks it's Morrison's fault. He broods about it for a while and decides to come back and really do a job?"

"I suppose so," Carlstrom said. He rubbed his hand across his mouth. "He said he was going to kill him. After he hit him. He used an ashtray."

Deglin opened his mouth a little and lifted his eyebrows. "Oh," he said. "You'd kind of overlooked that."

"Yes, sir."

"Did anyone else hear him say it?"

"I imagine so."

"This dame, Morgan. Did she hear it, do you think?"

"She was right there."

"What does she look like?"

"Good looking."

"This Paine. What does he look like? We might run into him some time."

Carlstrom was becoming more nervous. "About your size. Looks something like you."

"Dark. Not too tall," Deglin said. He smiled. "Lousy disposition."

NIGHT CRY

Riley started to smile too, then changed it to a chuckle. Deglin didn't say anything for a moment. He measured Carlstrom slowly until the man shifted and looked at Riley.

Riley regarded him with interest, and Carlstrom settled for a point halfway between them.

"This Paine," Deglin said. "How was he dressed?"

"Tweed coat. Flannels. Long tabbed sports shirt and a knit tie."

"He had a key for the joint?"

Carlstrom said nothing.

"What's his address? Where does he live?"

Carlstrom shrugged.

Deglin grunted. He leaned forward in his chair, pulled open Carlstrom's double-breasted dinner jacket, reached into the inside pocket and took from it a notebook. Carlstrom looked at him murderously.

"Maybe it isn't in here," Deglin said, giving him a bleak smile. He thumbed through the book slowly. Finally he paused, took a pad from his own pocket and noted a number on it. He tossed the notebook back to Carlstrom suddenly, so that it hit him and slid to the floor. Carlstrom recovered it. His face was white.

"Beat it," Deglin said. "Back in the room."

He watched Carlstrom get up and leave the small foyer. Riley watched also. Then he turned to Deglin.

"He's kind of a new one, Mark. Nervous type."

"Yeah," Deglin said. He looked down at the body of Morrison. In pulling it over so that they could see the face, they had twisted it so that the legs were crossed at the ankles. The heavy chin jutted into the air. Deglin studied it morosely.

"What about this guy Paine?" he said.

"He's been in the papers," Klein said.

"I'm hazy about it. Go ahead."

"Well, he was a hero. Knocked out a whole platoon of Germans someway—"

"Knife?" Deglin asked.

"Maybe. I don't remember," Klein said. "He got some important medals, and he's supposed to be writing a book."

"This'll put a rough end on the book," Deglin said.

He got to his feet and went into the gambling room. Riley and

Klein followed him. The quiet talk stopped again, abruptly. Smith looked up from a study of the roulette wheel, his face sharpening with interest. The men and women who had by now shifted their chairs until they were in small groups watched Deglin pick up a telephone and dial a number.

He looked at them and smiled. He said into the mouthpiece, loudly, "Put me through to Knight."

After a space, Knight's heavy voice said, "Yeah?"

"This is Deglin," Deglin said.

"Oh," Knight said. "How does it look? Shall I come down?"

"I don't think so," Deglin said. "We've got—" his eyes went over the group—"fourteen. Five women, three men, the manager, two dealers, and three waiters. Maybe the staff had time to clear out. Anyway, there's nobody in the kitchen."

"Look like much trouble?"

"No," Deglin said. "We've talked to the manager. He gave us some information. There's some smart kind of a kid involved. Big hero, likes to take punches at people. Except tonight he got knocked on his fanny."

"That was seen?"

"Probably by fourteen people," Deglin said. "His fight was with the dead man. They tossed him out, but he could have gotten back in."

"Don't they know? Don't they have a guy on the door?"

"It's a key club. He could have gone out, waited, then come back in and taken care of the guy who rapped him in the eye."

"Okay," said Knight. "Who is this character?"

"Name is Paine. Kendall Paine."

Knight's voice worried over it for a moment. "Haven't I heard of him?" he said finally.

"Yeah," Deglin said. "A hero of some kind. And the stiff is a rapid guy with a buck named L. O. Morrison."

Knight said nothing and Deglin, after shaking his head at Smith who had moved suddenly to his side, went on: "Riley is here from Homicide. He and Klein will cover the rest while I go after Paine."

"You think you can find him?" Knight asked.

"If I move fast."

"You'd better take Klein with you."

NIGHT CRY

"Look," Deglin said. "There're fourteen people here. They ought to be talked to right away. While they're still nervous." Knight was quiet and Deglin continued, "We'll want a wagon up here."

"All right," Knight said.

"And Klein'll check on the kitchen help. He'll get the Telegraph Bureau onto them."

"Okay," Knight said. "Let me talk to Riley."

Deglin held the receiver out to Riley and the big man came over and took it. "Hello, Al," he said. "Congratulations."

Deglin's eyes went to him briefly. He picked up his hat.

"I'll bring the kid to the station," he said to Klein. "You'll be done here."

Klein nodded. "You taking the cruiser?"

"You may need it."

Deglin put his hat on at the proper angle, glanced at the people seated near the roulette wheel and started out through the foyer. He stopped for a minute at the outer door as two young men, raincoats over their white uniforms, moved in with a stretcher.

"All right to take it?" one of them said.

Deglin nodded. They went by and he stepped out into the rain. A moment later, Smith followed him.

2

There was a tension in both the boy and the girl when they walked into the boy's room. He turned on the light, disclosing the disorder and grubbiness and, without saying anything, went to the plain varnished bureau and took from it a bottle of whisky. He turned and looked at her, as though daring her to object. His eyes were light and angry, and under one, where he had been struck, the swelling had already begun to discolor.

"Ken," she said.

"I'm going to have a drink."

"I didn't mean that." Her own eyes had darkened with annoyance. "I think we ought to fix your eye. It's going to look horrible."

He went to the mirror and leaned forward, peering at himself.

"The big mutt cut it a little bit," he said with surprise.

He followed her to the small bathroom, where she was looking through the medicine cabinet. He stood beside her, getting in her way until she said, "Sit down, Ken." Then he turned and lowered the seat and sat.

He held his face up so that she could work on his eye. He felt the sting of the alcohol in the small cut, the immediate coolness and wetness of the compress. She frowned slightly over the placement of the adhesive and finally remarked regretfully, "This one piece will be where the whiskers grow," and stuck it on.

"There," she said. But when he got suddenly to his feet and started to take her in his arms, she said again, with annoyance, "Please, Ken," and twisted away from him.

He followed her into the room, the anger again in his eyes.

"Well, what in the hell did you come here for?" he demanded bitterly.

She had walked to the back of the room, to a recess where a window overlooked a small courtyard. She stood there, her face turned to the window.

"Because I wanted to make sure you got home, Ken."

"Oh. So now I'm a no-good bum!"

"And because I wanted to talk to you."

She heard his footsteps as he went again to the bureau, then to the bathroom, the running of water in a glass and then the different sound of whisky being poured. Outside the window, in the pale light that flooded down from the room, the branches of a tree flung their few tattered leaves in the wind. She watched the branches whip in and out of the column of light.

"All right, Morgan," he said behind her.

"It's—it's no good anymore, Ken. No use trying."

"What do you mean?" he said. His tone had suddenly lost its anger. Instead, it was faintly amused. She was silent, trying to find some way to say that she had lost hope of ever finding in him that which had been promised by his charm and belied by his preoccupation with himself.

And when she didn't speak, he laughed behind her mockingly. "I know what you mean." When she felt his hands on her shoulders, she whirled suddenly and slapped him.

She stood backed against the sill, her eyes wide, as he put his hand to his cheek. The muscles of his face ridged under his tan and he turned and went to the front of the room.

"I know what you mean," he said doggedly. "You mean you're like everyone else. You mean that you can't stand the fact that young Kendall Paine, the guy that could do everything, has shown himself to be a guy who can't do anything.

"You mean that you're tired of all the brightness and gaiety, and now, since you're tired of it, *I've* got to settle down. It's time, you think, that the playing stopped and the working started, and since you think it, by God, I'd better do it or you're washed up."

"Ken," she said sharply.

He went on, the ridges still in his face, the bandage glowing white across the room: "It's inconceivable to you that I myself might hate this indecision, this fact that I can't settle down. You're like everyone else. You couldn't think of helping. If I can't do it for myself, I can damn soon sink to where I belong." He looked around the room. "And I'm doing a good job of it."

"But, Ken—" she began again.

"The hell with it," he said, his voice choked. "Let me alone."

She went to the door and went down the flight of stairs to the street. The misting rain cooled her face, and she stood for a moment, letting her cheeks become wet and cold. Then she walked through the darkness, slowly, turning aimlessly at corners, her young face white and intent.

Smith caught Deglin at the foot of the steps leading from the old brownstone. He walked with him to one of the patrol cars and waited as Deglin took the pad of paper from his pocket.

"Got your street guide?" Deglin said to the patrolman in the car.

The patrolman nodded, switched on an overhead light, and dug a dog-eared booklet from his pocket. The radio came on hoarsely and he listened attentively to the call until it went off.

"East Side," he said.

"I know," Deglin said and showed him the pad. "Where's this?"

The patrolman looked at it and thumbed through the book. "Down on the West Side about Tenth Street," he said. "Right at the river, Lieutenant. Artists and dock wallopers live there."

"Thanks," Deglin said.

He turned and walked to the corner and turned again, toward Broadway. Smith kept pace with him.

"All right if I go along with you on this, Mark?" he asked finally.

"No," Deglin said.

"If this kid did it, he's likely to be a little hasty." Smith said equably.

"He may have been a hero once," Deglin said. "He's a punk now. How many men do you need to take a punk?"

Smith said nothing, and because of that they walked rapidly in silence until he spoke again.

"This going to do you any good, Mark?" His voice was quiet.

"What're you talking about?"

Smith shrugged in the darkness.

Deglin went on, his voice edged, "Look, I'm the district man on this. It's my case. If it goes wrong, I get the eating out. Not Riley and not Knight."

"Yes," Smith said.

"What does Knight do? Get mad because I'm right?"

"No," Smith said. He let it go at that. On Broadway, at the subway

NIGHT CRY

entrance, he stopped at a newsstand and bought the morning tabloids, then clattered down the stairs after Deglin. He handed one of the papers to Deglin and they stood together, looking rapidly through the pages as an express thundered by and a local came gingerly to the platform and stopped.

They sat opposite a young couple. The girl was dark and pretty; the man young and animated. He said things in her ear and she looked at the car cards above Deglin's head and smiled. She looked at Deglin once with frank interest. After that she looked more attentively at the car cards, and smiled with even greater spontaneity. Deglin looked evenly at her until Smith, seeing that the young man had noticed and had stopped his own smiling and talking, put his hand on Deglin's arm.

Deglin turned his head and looked at him.

"Sure I can't go?"

Deglin nodded.

"It'd make a nice story," Smith said regretfully.

Deglin smiled, fleetingly. "Let's change to the local at Seventy-second Street," he said, and got to his feet. "You'll be getting off at Fifty-ninth."

"Okay," Smith said.

On the local, Deglin looked at his tabloid. At once he said with exasperation, "Where do these columnists get their stuff about me?"

"You give it to them," Smith said.

"Not this," Deglin said.

He handed the tabloid to Smith and Smith read an item which said that the seamy side of the underworld would be steering clear of Mark Deglin, the Mister Tough of the plainclothes men. "He'll be taking it out on them for what he didn't get in the recent Civil Service advances," it concluded.

"Well?" Smith said.

Deglin laughed shortly.

As the train slowed for 59th Street, Smith got to his feet and looked at his watch. "You needn't hurry the solution, Mark. It's a little late for the morning papers anyway." He grinned.

Deglin nodded. He watched Smith crowd his way to the end door of the car. When the train stopped and the door slid open, Smith stepped through. Deglin watched the sudden influx of passengers for a moment. Then, while they still fought the doors back and crowded in, he fell to brooding over the item.

The Mister Tough . . . the guy who could go out and get them and bring them in . . . but the guy who was passed over . . . three years of waiting, just to be passed over, and in another year, the whole thing to go through again—the cramming for the exams—the hot sweaty room—the big, intent men placed carefully like school kids, with vacant desks in between....

He crumpled the paper in his hands.

At Fourteenth, the rain had slackened temporarily, though the wind still whipped the streets. Several all-night restaurants and a small nest of bars threw a bright glare across the wet pavements. Traffic lights gleamed green and then red up and down Seventh Avenue while Deglin lit a cigarette. A late cab splashed to a stop. Inside it, someone was lighting a cigarette, too, and the flame glowed on the face of a girl laughing with careless good humor.

Deglin turned to the west, toward the Hudson. He walked purposefully, his hands deep in the pockets of his raincoat. For a short while the lights glowed warmly in the buildings and the doors opened often. Young men and women came through them laughing to one another, or back at those whom they were leaving, saying quick things that were caught by the wind. After those blocks there were fewer lights. The soft complaints of the river traffic grew until, as Deglin passed under the New York Central tracks that wandered down the shore, he heard only the sounds of the wind and the deep, empty whistles, and his own footsteps.

He walked clear to the river street and stood there for a moment, enjoying the melancholy of it. It was starkly empty. Overhead, the elevated highway, gigantic on its steel legs, crawled to the right and left. Up river and down the pier buildings sat, dark and silent. Directly across, two naked bulbs burned bleakly outside the entrances to the ferry and inside the ferry building itself the red of an automobile taillight reflected dully. Over it all was the new varnish of the rain, catching the few lights and reflecting them a hundred-fold.

The rain came again, first from the river which he could see through a slip next to the ferry, then across the wide street. He

NIGHT CRY 37

turned his back to it and went the few yards to a short street that paralleled the river. It was a block long—a short block. Lights showed at intervals in the buildings and he went the length twice before he found the address he wanted. It had been reconstructed in a way. The paint was fresh, but it covered only irregularities of the weather-chewed brownstone and the rusted iron palings on the narrow porch.

The tiny foyer of the building was unlighted. Deglin could see that there were mailboxes and that they had names. But there were no bells. He pushed at the door and it opened on a dimly illuminated lower hall. To his left, a door bore a small celluloid card upon which was printed, "J. Metaxa." He walked up the narrow stairs. There was a string of light under the door. The name plate said, "K. Paine." He rapped once, then again, more sharply.

For a space, there was no sound. Then Deglin heard a floor board creak, and a voice said, "Come in."

He pushed the door open.

Paine was standing at the bed, leaning slightly over it, his head turned toward the door. He wore a bandage over his left eye. It was startlingly white against his tan skin. In addition, there was an angry scratch across his right cheek. He was Deglin's height.

"What do you want?" he said. His voice was thick. It trembled slightly as though he were in a rage.

"Just want to talk," Deglin said.

"About what?"

Deglin walked in. The room was small. Two normal-sized windows virtually filled the front wall. There was another window in a recess in the back wall. There were two chairs and the bed. A plain desk, and a plain bureau with the drawers pulled open. There was a bottle of whisky on the bureau. A glass half full sat on the desk beside the bed. A closet door was also open—a large closet. On the bed in front of Paine, there was a brown canvas kitbag with some shirts stacked beside it. On the bag was stenciled, "Lt. K. B. Paine," and a number.

Deglin sat down in one of the chairs.

"Going someplace?" he said.

Paine wrinkled up his eye and shook his head. He licked his lips twice.

"Wrong guy," he said. "Get outa here."

"What do you mean, wrong guy?" Deglin said.

"You're not anyone I know," Paine said. "Beat it."

Deglin smiled at him. "That's right," he said. He put his hat, which was quite wet, on the floor beside the chair. "But I'm staying. I'd like to talk to you."

Paine sat on the edge of the bed. "With this one covered up," he indicated his left eye, "and with this," he motioned at the glass of whisky, "I don't see too well. But now I see you and I want you to get the hell outa here."

"In time," Deglin said. "First, sonny, how long you been in here?"

"Why?"

Deglin reached into his pocket and got out his badge. "This is why."

Paine shrugged. "You know what you can do with that?" he said. "Well do it. Outside."

Deglin's face tightened. "That's right," he said softly. "I forgot you were a hero. Look, hero, it's important around New York when someone dies."

"All right," Paine said. "Drop dead."

"How long have you been here?" Deglin said.

"An hour," Paine said.

"You were thrown out of a joint up on Riverside Drive an hour ago."

"All right. An hour minus whatever it took me to get home. Good God." Paine moved restlessly on the bed. "Get on with it," he said.

"Where were you going?" Deglin said, motioning to the bag.

"Away. I don't know." Paine grimaced and spread his hands out. "I got a headache," he said. "I don't feel good. Will you quit stalling around and let me alone?"

"So you can go wherever you're going?" Deglin asked.

"Yeah, if you want it that way. Any way you want it. So I can go wherever I'm going. So I can go flying around the moon or swimming in the goddamn Hellespont or canoeing at Canoe Brook or—" he stopped and shook his head.

"Did you knife those Japs," Deglin said.

Paine rubbed his neck. "What Japs?"

"All those Japs you killed?"

NIGHT CRY

"They weren't Japs. They were Krauts."

"Did you knife them, too?"

"I knifed them, and I choked them and—what the hell are talking about?" he lifted his head, quickly.

"That knife in Morrison," Deglin snapped.

"What in the hell—"

"You got a key to that joint?"

"I—" He rubbed his hand across his face.

Deglin looked at him steadily. "You get in a lot of trouble," he said. "Where did you get that?"

"At the club," Paine said quickly.

Deglin grunted. "You were hit only once. In the eye. Where did you get it?"

Paine said nothing.

"Where's the dame?" Deglin said. "Maybe she could tell us what you've been doing. Maybe she could tell us when you went back and stuck Morrison. I think you went back and stuck him and that's where you got that scratch."

Paine took a step forward, his face working. Deglin got to his feet quickly, so that he stood directly in front of Paine.

"Morrison's dead?" Paine said.

Deglin nodded. He put his left hand out and put it on Paine's right shoulder. "Yes," he said.

Paine slapped his hand away. "Get your damn hands away." His voice was high and tight.

Deglin backhanded him across the face. "You cheap punk," he said.

Paine stared at him, his one eye wide, his face mottling with anger. He stepped forward, his arms out. Deglin feinted at the eye and when the arms came up, he hit Paine in the belly. Paine shuddered and Deglin hit him, as hard as he could hit, in the face on the blind side, then chopped at Paine's neck. Paine started to buckle forward. Deglin hit him again, savagely, and again chopped at his neck. The blows turned Paine and carried him back onto the bed. He lay for a moment, breathing rapidly in choking gasps, then he floundered awkwardly and slid to the floor. The rapid breathing stopped.

Deglin kneaded his own left hand with his right for a moment, then looked at it. The knuckles were bruised. He clenched and unclenched his fist, his jaw muscle jumping.

"Punk," he said again, softly.

He reached down and took Paine by the shoulders and pulled him up. "Okay, hero," he said. "We're going in."

Paine's one eye was half open. His head lolled. For an instant Deglin held him erect. Then he let go and Paine slumped again, his head hitting the floor sharply. Deglin picked up Paine's wrist and held it. Then he opened the shirt and shoved his hand in against the hairy chest. He stood up suddenly and looked down, his jaw muscles flickering again. He began to knead his knuckles, first those of the left hand, then those of the right.

He went to a chair and sat in it, avoiding the sight of Paine, glancing at other things in the room. He wasn't worried. But he didn't like it. He'd never done this before, actually killed a man, so quickly and easily. Maybe the guy had heart trouble—or maybe he'd broken the neck when he chopped at it the second time. He sat for a minute getting used to it. Presently, he got to his feet again. He remembered the pay phone in the hall and went out to it. He fumbled through his pockets for a nickel and finding he had none, slid a dime into the slot. It dinged twice, sharply, and the buzz in the receiver started. It all happened slowly and distinctly while he kept trying to think. But it was as though his mind, shocked beyond his own immediate shock, had stopped of itself. He had no thoughts particularly. He was in an odd position; that was the way this self apart from himself put it. The detached self was slightly sardonic but he wasn't. He dialed the number and he told the voice he wanted to talk to Knight. Knight came on and said, "Hello?"

"It's Deglin," Deglin said. His voice sounded rough and ragged.

"Yeah," Knight said. "Wait till I close this damn door." The receiver hummed for an instant and he came back. "Yeah, Mark?" he said. "Jesus, they just got in and they're talking their heads off."

"I'm up at Paine's," Deglin said carefully.

"We'll want him if he saw anything. Just a statement, tell him," Knight said.

"What?" Deglin said.

"Just a statement," Knight said. He was in a good humor. "Go on

NIGHT CRY

home."

"I can't," Deglin said.

"The hell you can't," Knight said. "The case is closed. It was Carlstrom. Morrison had lost about five gees to the syndicate and he kept laughing off Carlstrom when he put the bite on him. Carlstrom got mad out in the foyer, that's all."

"How did you break it?"

Knight laughed. "Riley and Klein turn up the fact that Carlstrom takes Morrison out of the room. One of the house men drops the fact that Morrison is on the hook for the money. One of the women notices that Carlstrom is very nervous when he comes back."

"Yes."

"Well, he got panicky and broke for a back door. Riley nailed him under the shoulder. Then, in the ambulance on the way to the hospital Riley convinced him he was going die. Carlstrom broke up."

"I see," Deglin said.

"His name is really Carlstrom," Knight added. "Italian mother."

"Oh," Deglin said. He waited.

"Say, Mark," Knight said, "there's no one in here. I could talk to you about this tomorrow but what the hell. I saw those gossip columns."

Deglin said nothing. He was again seeing Paine flounder off the bed, again hearing the choking gasps.

"Damn it," Knight said, "I'd hate to think that you were taking this hard. I didn't have a damn thing to do with getting this."

"I know," Deglin said.

"We'll get along," Knight said. "Christ, you'll be an inspector before I will."

"Thanks," Deglin said.

"The kid all right?" Knight asked more conversationally.

Deglin stood at the phone. His jaw twitched and he put his free hand to it. He wet his lips with his tongue. "I think he's cleared out," he said suddenly.

Knight grunted.

"I don't know," Deglin said. "I got into his room. The bathroom stuff was gone. And most of his clothes."

"What the hell," Knight said thoughtfully.

"Have you put out an alarm on him yet?"

"No," Knight said. "This other thing broke too fast."

"I'll do it," Deglin said. "I've got a good description."

"Okay," Knight said. "What time you coming in tomorrow?"

"Early," Deglin said.

Knight's voice said, "Get some sleep." There was a click and the receiver hummed emptily.

Deglin pulled the phone arm down with his forefinger and the dime dropped inside the case. He dropped another dime and it dinged twice. He dialed.

To the bored woman who answered, he said, "Is Miss Corby on?"

"She's on," she said.

"Will you tell her that Mr. Deglin called?"

"Oh, hello, Mr. Deglin," the woman said.

"Hello," Deglin said. "Tell her that I'm tied up. I can't meet her. I'll call her, maybe tomorrow."

"Sure," the woman said, and Deglin put the receiver back.

He went back into Paine's room.

"You've cleared out, kid," he said softly to the body on the floor. He sat down on the chair to think but he found he wasn't doing it too well. Outside, the rain drummed nervously against the window. Boat noises drifted into the room, remote and muffled, but lonesome. There was no other sound but his own breathing and it was unaccountably loud. He was aware of the body. He could sit beside other bodies and be completely indifferent to them, but he was aware of Paine.

The awareness stung him to activity. He crossed to the bed and went through Paine's pockets. There was a wallet. It contained a driver's license and some identification cards. There was no money. In addition, there was an address book and the return half of a round-trip ticket to Greenwich, Connecticut. In Paine's pants' pocket, Deglin found a bunch of keys, seventy-three cents in change and a handkerchief. He guessed that one of the keys was for the small apartment and one for the gambling club. The others might have been for anything at all; he would never know. He put the keys and the address book, the ticket and the change in his pocket.

He went back to the chair and sat, looking at the body for a moment. He thought to himself, without any particular emotion,

NIGHT CRY

that he had killed a man.

When was the first time he had ever seen a man dead? Long ago. Twenty-five years ago, when they had taken the suicide from the flat above his mother's. He had been a kid. Twelve? Maybe thirteen. And he had expected, as he hung quietly behind the police, to see something dread and obscene. But the old man had been neither. The face had been pale and tired, and the clothes had seemed to belong to someone else the way they fitted the slumped body, though they had always looked all right before. That was all.

And how many dead had he seen since? A thousand? Perhaps. But this was the first person he had killed himself. He'd beaten many men and a couple of women. But this was the first dead one.

Deglin got to his feet impatiently. He was a damn fool to have said Paine was gone. He should have said Paine had put up a fight and he'd had to knock him out. Still drunk. Feeling scrappy. That was Paine.

"He looks bad, Knight," he should have said. "I'm a little worried."

"I'll get the medics over," Knight would have said.

And they would have come over and there would have been a stink, but it would have been over. Over? Until the next time they looked at the Civil Service eligibility lists. And there would be Deglin's name and it wouldn't be over after all. It would only be starting.

No, Paine had cleared out. That had to be it. Paine had to vanish— and someone had to see him in the act of vanishing. Paine had to be seen making those last few movements that would establish his disappearance as real and acceptable.

Deglin went to the body beside the bed. He began to strip it. The grey flannels and the soft tweed jacket, the long tabbed, rolling collar and the knit tie knotted loosely. They were distinctive. The raincoat thrown over the chair and still damp from the rain was an officer's coat. This, and the snap-brim hat, and the officer's kitbag with Paine's stenciled name fading on the side. This was the logical thing.

There was no more need for Paine. He would go for a trip and not come back, and though some might wonder, no one would know. The police would not care. Deglin was on the case. Paine was out of it.

Deglin moved more quickly. The grey flannels and the tweed looked good, and when he knotted the tie under the wings of the soft collar, it looked like it had looked on Paine. He folded his own clothes, carefully put them in the partially packed bag, even his hat. He went through the bureau drawers quickly. There was nothing Paine would have needed. He went into the bathroom and found Paine's shaving kit and toothbrush and put those in the bag, too.

He finally went through the small desk. There were some assorted pages of handwritten manuscript in a drawer, notes and character sketches, and a notebook of the type stenographers use was filled with closely written pages. He put those in the bag. And finally, on top of the desk, there was an unstamped, sealed envelope addressed to a Mrs. John Leming in Parsonville, Mass. Deglin put it in the bag.

After he had pulled Paine's body into the closet and closed the door, he strapped the bag shut. He went to the bathroom mirror and checked the appearance of the bandage he had put over his left eye. It was the one Paine had worn, and he was momentarily afraid that it might not stick properly. He cut another piece of adhesive and applied it.

At the door, he looked carefully around the room. He should take care of Paine's body first, he thought. It would be better. But it would have to wait. His eyes caught a thing he had not noticed, and he went to an ashtray and picked up a stubbed cigarette. The end was carmine and when he touched it the color came off on his fingers. The girl had been there that night. He snapped off the light.

Outside, the wind had fallen and the rain was different. It came in a mist-like drift and with it a chill fog moved slowly. Deglin waited on the stoop. There was a faint luminescence to the rain itself although the short street was dark. Directly across the way, on the second floor, a single window glowed. Deglin wondered suddenly if the shades in Paine's apartment had been up or down, and couldn't remember. He looked across at the window. There was a form faintly outlined behind the curtain but it didn't move and Deglin, with only one eye, couldn't tell whether it was at the window or back from it. He turned up the collar of the raincoat and went down the three steps to the sidewalk, thinking of the shades and, with annoyance, of Paine's hat. It was a trifle too small for him. It felt alien, and the tightness made him uncomfortable and unsure of himself.

He walked to the darker corner toward the north and then turned away from the river toward the Village.

Except for the misting rain, the street lay quiet and deserted. The voices of the ships on the river had become more insistent with the growing fog, but their sound was a muffled echo. The minutes passed. And finally, the figure at the second-floor window, which had been so motionless, stirred slowly. It retreated from the window and, after a space, the soft yellow light that had framed it, disappeared. Then the street was completely without life for a time. A half hour passed and the wind and rain freshened again. Then silence was broken as a large figure turned into the street and hurried along, head bent. Heels clacked against the wet pavement and changed sound on the three stairs to Paine's building. The big young man pushed the door to the vestibule open and went up the flight of stairs to Paine's apartment. He was slightly and pleasantly drunk. He hummed something under his breath. He rapped the door with his knuckles and waited, then he rapped again and said, "Hey, Ken. Open up."

There was still no sound. He tried the door and it opened under his hand. He went into the room slowly and found the light. When he had turned it on, he looked around with some puzzlement. Then he shrugged, turned out the light, closed the door behind him, and clattered back down the stairs and out into the rain.

3

Although the air that moved gustily through the half-opened bedroom window was cold, Knight perspired slightly under the covers. Yet he lay without moving, enduring the discomfort, staring up into the darkness. His wife lay next to him on her side, breathing heavily. Her soft buttock pressed against his leg, creating a spot of even greater warmth. Years before, the pressure of her body like that had created an almost insatiable desire in him. Now his feeling was a gentle possessiveness of which he was hardly aware.

He wondered what time it was and considered turning on the lamp to look at the alarm clock which ticked insistently across the room. But he knew that, although he felt it was very late, it was not more than one-thirty. He tried to clear his mind of its flying, pointless thoughts, but they ran through it quickly, aimlessly. If he could pin one down—one in which he was playing pinochle, or bowling, one with a monotonous regularity—he knew he could sleep. But he could not and he tortured himself instead by refusing to move. Then one of his legs jumped nervously and Madge's heavy breathing quieted. She did not move but he knew she had awakened. "Having a hell of a time," he rumbled softly.

"You haven't moved much," she said sleepily.

"I'd like to read, but my eyes sting," he said.

She turned in the bed, onto her back, and he moved with sudden violence.

"Can I get you some milk, Al?" she asked. "Sometimes that'll help."

"Naw," he said.

He lay still again, his thoughts quieter now that she was awake.

"Still raining?" she asked.

He knew it needed no answer. He gave none. And after another minute, she said softly, "Thinking about Deglin, Al?"

"I sure wish he wouldn't be so down on me," he said heavily.

"But you didn't have any say in it, Al," she said reasonably. "He'll get

NIGHT CRY

over it. Others have been passed over. Why, *you* were passed over!"

"But it's hard for Deglin," Knight said slowly. "He's come fast until now. He doesn't do things by the book all the time but he's smart. He doesn't think much of doing things by the book."

"Oh, for goodness' sake," she said with exasperation. "You'd think Mark Deglin was a special kind of something."

Knight lay, thinking of words. "Well," he began slowly, "I guess maybe he is. Mark is a live kind of a guy. The brass that goes over the eligibility lists, maybe they don't see that. Maybe they only see where he didn't do this or that according to Hoyle and they say, 'Hell, he's a big stylist.' But I gotta keep my guys on the ball. If he kinda goes against me and the others see it, maybe they'll think they can too. Klein, Corrigan, they think he's got a light bulb in his ass. And Riley. Remember Dan Riley?"

"Yes," she said sleepily.

"He's in Homicide now, down on Twentieth. *He* thinks anything Mark does is perfect."

"Why don't you talk to Deglin?" she asked.

"I did, sort of. Over the phone. He sounded all right." His voice puzzled over the fact.

"Sure," she said comfortably. "Why not? He can make it hard for you but you can make a whole hell of a lot of trouble for him. You're the boss, Al," she said.

He stared into the darkness, listening to the clock.

"Sure you don't want some hot milk?" she asked.

"Thanks," he said. "Don't think so. I'll get it if I do."

She turned on her side again and pulled the covers up strongly. The curtains flapped as the wind freshened outside. Knight looked into the darkness. Already his mind was framing another talk with Deglin. Maybe the first thing in the morning. He would call him in right away. He'd motion him into the chair opposite his desk and push a cigar across to him. No, the hell with the cigar. He'd say, "Mark, we've both got something on our minds. Let's get it off."

The thoughts blended together—the thoughts becoming dreams. He hardly heard Madge tell him urgently to turn over on his side. He was telling Mark Deglin things about the way the district had to go and Deglin's dark head was nodding, his dark eyes were interested and sympathetic.

4

The rain neither increased nor lessened in the hours of the night. The fog moved silently in from the river, clouding the short dark street near the waterfront, obscuring it, so that when Deglin came back to it, his passing could be noted only by his footsteps. He wore his own clothes and he did not carry the kitbag.

He moved up the steps, into the house. Upstairs, in the darkened room, he saw with relief that the shades were drawn. He moved silently, pausing occasionally to light a match and check his movements. When he had lit one, he blew it out and waited until the glow died; then put the expended pasteboard in his pocket. The only sounds were brief ones: the tiny screech of nails being pried from wood, and the heavier tapping as he forced the sash of the rear window back into its place.

He was busy for about twenty minutes. Not more than that. When he had finished, the room seemed as it had been before, except that the manager of the building would eventually be puzzled at the oddity of the things which Kendall Paine had chosen to take with him when he went away so suddenly—a spare blanket that had been stored in the closet, and the sashweights from the small window that overlooked the tiny court in the rear.

When the street door of the building opened, it remained slightly ajar for several minutes before Deglin reappeared through it. He stood in the darkness, breathing slowly through his mouth, listening intently. He had to turn his back to the door and back out in order to pull the limp, blanket-shrouded figure through the door, then he ducked quickly, and in the fog the two figures blended together.

He raised himself erect with a sudden upward thrust, and Paine's body was over his shoulders. He scuttered across the street into deep shadow, and moved more quietly to the south, next to the building. At the corner, he turned to the river. The sounds of the fog horns grew heavier, some dulled by the distance, one deep and close, but moving up-river. There was no sound on the street. Under

NIGHT CRY 49

the rows of pillars that towered above him to support the elevated highway, he carried Paine, cautiously moving from pillar to pillar, until he had passed the faint glow in the fog that indicated the ferry building. There was no activity, just the slow sound of water against the pilings. He angled across, moving more slowly, feeling his way, until abruptly he came to the wooden abutment of the slip. He let Paine down softly then, and crouched. He opened his mouth to quiet the sound of his heavy breathing.

The slow swell of the river sucked against the pilings and from the luminous darkness of the water there came a steady, and even creaking. That would be tugs tied up, he told himself. He checked the wire around the blanketed body, pulled sharply at the heavy sashweights. They were firm. Then he rolled the body up on a timber and let it go. He was hardly able to hear the soft plunge. The slow hissing of the bubbles blended with the hiss of the rain and the steady sucking of the waves.

He crouched for a moment, listening. Then he moved off into the fog.

Three-quarters of an hour later, he let himself out of the automatic elevator in his apartment building and into his own small suite. He flipped a wall switch and two lamps that flanked a long upholstered couch glowed. The room was rather large, and furnished modestly but with excellent taste. On one side, two large windows and a door opened on a balcony. Outside, and down eighteen floors, under the fog and rain, the East River moved slowly.

He stood for a moment in the center of the floor, chewing at his lip, his eyes squinted. Then he moved to the tiny kitchen and, opening one of the cupboards, took out a bottle of whisky and poured half a glass. He shuddered slightly after he had drained it. He ran a little water into the glass. This he sipped.

He went to his bedroom and turned on the light. It was a small room. He had cursed its smallness before and now he cursed it again. Against the wall the kitbag stood, the stenciled name clear. He opened the wardrobe impatiently and looked back at the bag. He had already tried that. It had not fit before. It wouldn't fit now. He went into the living room, surveying each corner, each piece of furniture. When he returned to the bedroom, he turned the bag so that the name was to the wall. Then he turned out the light.

In the living room, he sat down without taking off his rain coat or his hat. His hands jumped in his lap and he rubbed his knuckles. Those of his left were still tender. He rubbed his jaw and got quickly to his feet. He went to the kitchen and poured another half tumbler of whisky. He downed it, poured more into the glass and carried it back to the room with him. He couldn't think what to do with the bag. He'd tried at New Rochelle to dump it, but every son-of-a-bitch in New Rochelle had seemed to be running around in the rain. He'd had it cram it into the phone booth with him at 125th Street, when he finally called the Telegraph Bureau and gave them the alarm on Paine. He'd had to bring it with him, all the way, hanging onto the goddamn thing as though it held a ton of gold instead of forty pounds of death. He'd have to get rid of it, some way. He couldn't have it kicking around. He finished his drink abruptly and returned to the bedroom, unstrapped the bag and took from it the unstamped, sealed envelope and the address book. He worked for a while over the envelope in the kitchen, pausing now and then to have another sip of whisky, until he finally had it open. He read the letter inside hurriedly.

Dear Sis: I've torn it with Morgan, but mostly with myself. I know that my last letter must have concerned you, and your usually sound advice that I should take stock of myself is unsound only because, upon doing so, I feel at a lower ebb than ever.

It is ridiculous to suppose that anyone—even Morgan— could be aware of what the last five years of batting around has done to my equilibrium. Anything that even smacks of ease and contentment is anathema to me; I am a toppling man. But then, by the same token, it is ridiculous to be in this state.

I'm a little in the bag at the moment—regrettably. I may take a crack at seeing Morgan again and patching things up or I may not. But I'm going to do something. I hope, dear, it turns out right.

love,
Ken

NIGHT CRY   **51**

Deglin's lips tightened faintly and he frowned as he went to the desk, glued the flap of the envelope carefully back in place, and stamped it. He then went through the address book slowly, finally stopping. He smiled for the first time, thinly. The name was Morgan Taylor. The address: Whiteoaks, Greenwich.

He put the stamped letter in his pocket, switched off the living room lights, and left the apartment.

Fifteen minutes later, ten blocks downtown, his raincoat again wet from the rain, he let himself into a gold and grey apartment with a key he had on his chain. With the familiarity that came of having been in the room often, he moved to a small table and turned on a single soft light. He took off his hat and raincoat and dropped them on a grey leather chair. There was a crystal flask of whisky on a low cabinet beside a deep chair. He poured some into a glass he took from the cabinet, and sat in the chair, his head against the back. After a moment, he straightened, got a cigarette, and lit it. He breathed deeply of the smoke and lay back again. He stayed that way for some time. He heard the door open behind him but he paid no attention. His second cigarette was burning between his fingers and he raised it and pulled on it with his eyes closed.

"Hello, Mark," the voice said.

"Hello, Jane," he answered.

She came into the room. She had been asleep, but she was still beautiful. She was a blonde but she would have been lovely as a brunette or a redhead. She was wearing heavy silk pajamas and she hadn't put on a robe over them. Her feet were bare. She was slender, with a rather long face, and narrow feet and hands. Her eyes were dark and long. She sat on the arm of Deglin's chair and he put a hand on her thigh.

"Are you drunk?" she asked.

He shook his head.

"I got your message," she said. "I was tired, so I came on home and went to bed." She stretched luxuriously. "God, I've slept," she said.

"Good," Mark said. He raised his head to sip from the glass and lay back again. "You're good for me, baby," he said.

"Not tonight," she said, laughing. "I've got an early date. Recording."

Deglin smiled, his eyes closed.

"You're feeling better about things, aren't you, Mark," she said gently.

The smile faded from his lips but he nodded.

"I'm glad," she said. "I was worried that you were so bitter. I don't like you so much when you're bitter, honey."

"When do you like me, Janie?" His voice was drowsy and his body was slack in the chair.

"When you're Mark Deglin."

"That's me."

She waited a minute and said more softly, as though not to him at all, "When you're kind of amused . . . and kind of tough . . . and kind of gentle."

"Gentle!"

She laughed again. "You're gentle, Mark. Sometimes."

"I think I can sleep," he said.

She sat quietly, looking down at him. In the warm light, his face was brown and worn. She ran a finger over his eyelids then loosened the knit tie he was wearing and unbuttoned his collar.

"I like the shirt, Mark," she said lazily.

Deglin's eyes opened and he looked briefly at the meeting of ceiling and wall lost in the shadows, as memories of Paine came surging back.

"I don't," he said. "I don't wear it often."

She put her arm around the back of the chair and moved her fingers along his cheek until his eyes closed again.

When the muscles of his face and body had finally slackened and she knew he was approaching sleep, she slipped her arm carefully from around his shoulders and stood, looking down at him. Then she dropped to her knees and began to untie his shoelaces. His shoes were wet and she said to herself with compassion, "The damn fool."

Deglin stirred suddenly and she stopped worrying his shoe. He threw his head back as if in distress, and held it there stiffly. He said something rapidly, the words lost in his throat. She was arrested by the pain in his face and she put her hand on his arm. He awakened instantly.

"I think you're catching cold, Mark," she said.

Deglin sat forward and shook his head. He kneaded the back of his neck with his hand, then rubbed his face.

"You were talking in your sleep," she said.

He raised his face, startled. "Talking?"

"I couldn't tell what you said," she murmured.

He got to his feet and, noticing the untied shoe, crouched to tie it. He still looked at her.

"I'll have to get back to the apartment, Jane," he said quickly. "I'll have to change before I go into the office tomorrow."

She watched him get his raincoat and shrug into it. He picked up his hat.

"You ought to take a hot tub, and some aspirin, Mark," she said.

He looked for his hat and found it. "I will, honey," he said abstractedly. He left without kissing her.

5

The morning was drab and cold. Rain was torn from the low scurrying clouds in sudden thin gusts. Deglin had breakfast in a corner restaurant, bright with light and warmth, and then went into a barbershop next door for a shave. He closed his aching eyes gratefully under the hot towel and rested as the barber rubbed warm soapsuds into his beard. When he had finished and sat up in the chair so that he could see himself in the mirror, Deglin decided he looked better. Though his eyes were puffy, the shock of the cold towel had taken some of the greyness from his face. He got out of the chair and looked at himself closely as he knotted his tie and pulled it up under the collar.

"Okay, Tony," he said and handed him a dime. Then he paid the bill and went on out and got into a cab.

He stopped the cab on Broadway, paid off the driver, and bought the last editions of the morning papers. He stood for a moment, looking through one, but the wind streaming up from Times Square rattled the pages in his hands. He folded them again and walked across, past Eighth Avenue, to the grey modern station house.

At the desk a uniformed cop was working at a typewriter. Deglin stopped and looked at the long stream of paper that ribboned out of the teletype. It clattered suddenly as he read and he watched the cryptic message appear. It was a holdup on the East Side, so he dismissed it from his mind and turned and went on upstairs.

The detective's waiting room was brilliantly lighted. Two men were at desks set back-to-back, laboring over reports. They nodded to Deglin and went on with their slow typing.

"Riley been in?" Deglin asked.

"He called from Twentieth Street," one of them said. "He'll be up. He wanted to know about the DA and the testimony."

"Anything else?"

"Knight's in already. Said when you come in to go on over."

Deglin took off his topcoat and hung it with his hat in the coat

NIGHT CRY

room. On the way across the hall to Knight's office, he lit a cigarette. When he pushed open the inner door, smoke was streaming from his nostrils.

There was a plainclothesman sitting across the desk from the large, grey-haired man, but Deglin went on in and moved across the office to the window. He looked out at the leaden sky until the detective had finished his report, then he turned back and sat against the window ledge.

"How are ya, Marty?" he said.

The detective grinned and went out. Knight turned in his chair so he faced Deglin.

"You look like I feel," Deglin said.

Knight nodded his head. "No sleep," he said, sighing. "I'd give an arm for about twenty straight hours." He eyed Deglin with interest. "You got insomnia, too, Mark?"

Deglin smiled. "Catching a cold. Gumshoeing around in the rain last night. No rubbers."

"You need a wife," Knight said. He was silent for a minute. "One thing Madge does is watch those things," he added.

Deglin waited during the silence that followed. "What's on your mind, Al?" he said finally.

Knight started to say something. He looked off at one of the walls, framing the words. Then he scowled with irritation and shrugged. "Nothing," he said. "Forget it."

"Okay," Deglin said. "How tight do you have Carlstrom pinned down?"

"He killed him all right."

Deglin put out his cigarette, got another out of his pocket and turned it in his fingers. "Brother," he said, "I had the wrong steer on that one." He lifted his head and grinned at Knight and Knight grinned back.

"Anyone see Carlstrom do it?"

"Nope," Knight said. "I've talked to the DA's office already. They guess that Paine saw it. That's why he cleared out."

"He's really gone?" Deglin asked.

"I called the precinct down there this morning. Had one of the boys drop over." Knight opened one of a dozen blue-covered folders on his desk and took out a piece of paper and studied it. "Most of his clothes gone, probably all he could get in a bag, also a bunch of papers, also all his bathroom stuff. Superintendent of the building says he always kept a big bag—kind officers carry—got his name on it—half packed in the room. He told the boys about the papers, too. Writing a book I guess." He put the paper back and lifted out a letter. "Found this in a drawer." He handed it over to Deglin.

It was a note in a square handwriting. Deglin turned the small page over. It was signed Morgan. It said, "I think your suggestion is a very pleasant one. I've told mother and father about you and they are very anxious to have you up for the evening. Dad will bore you to tears telling you about the first war, but I shall be very kind and not say a thing about the second. Then you won't have to talk at all. Won't it be nice?"

He turned it back and looked at the address on the front. "Whiteoaks, Greenwich. Sounds like an estate," he said.

Knight agreed. "Here's the envelope. Dated about a year ago. It's probably the dame with him at the gambling joint."

Deglin asked, "The DA's office really wants the kid?"

"On the chance he saw something."

"Riley will be here right away," Deglin said. "It shouldn't be hard."

Knight looked his pleasure. "I put out a teletype a while ago. They're checking cabs. With a big suitcase, he probably took a cab. I'll call you when something comes in."

Deglin got up from the window again and went to the door. "If Riley's here, I think we'll grab some coffee, Al," he said. "Back in about ten minutes."

"Okay, Mark," Knight said.

He looked at the door after Deglin had closed it, then he turned and looked out the window, pleased with himself. If I'd started shooting off my mouth about cooperation and the rest of that, I'd a spoiled the whole thing, he thought. Then he turned back to his desk.

Deglin and Riley spent fifteen minutes over coffee, Deglin nodding his head and grinning as Riley retold Carlstrom's confession.

"There was a scared Dago," Riley said, finishing. "One thing about killers, they almost always make a break for it—always gotta run. Ever notice that, Mark?"

Deglin grinned and nodded his head.

NIGHT CRY

Knight called him and Riley in after about a half hour. When they got to his office, a plainclothesman named Candido from a precinct in the Bronx was over at the window. He was looking at a cab driver who sat in the chair opposite Knight, and he was saying, "This is Mr. Gold, chief. He got outa bed to come over. I told him we'd be done with him in a shake."

"Yes, sir, inspector," the cab driver said. "Anything to help you guys out. I ain't like a lot of the hackies."

"Good," Knight said. "I understand you picked up a fare about one o'clock last night, down in the Village?"

"Yes, sir. Like I told the gentleman." The cabbie turned his head to Candido.

Knight took some pictures from his desk and handed them to the cab driver. "Any of these the man?" he asked.

The cabbie examined them one after the other, pursing his heavy lips. Then he shrugged. "It was night," he explained.

"But none of these men look like him?"

The cabbie looked again at the pictures. "Well, this one—or this one," he said, handing two back.

Knight nodded.

"Where did you take him?" Riley said.

The cabbie turned around in his chair.

"First he wanted to go to Grand Central, then he changed his mind and said a Hundred and Twenty-fifth Street station. Said something about getting some coffee."

"Where'd you pick him up?" Knight asked.

"On Tenth Street, near Seventh. I took him right up. Not much traffic."

"Thanks a lot, Mr. Gold," Knight said. "You've been very helpful."

Gold's eyes widened. "That's all?" he asked with some disappointment.

"Unless you have something more," Knight said.

"Sure," Gold said, settling back. "I have a little exchange of words with him which tells me he'd been in a fight."

"How's that?" Deglin asked.

"I am turning off on a side street to get over to Park and he asks when they're getting some Irish cab drivers. I say to him, 'You Irish?' and he says back that he's English. Then I say, 'You must have tied up with an Irishman with that eye.'" Gold chuckled. "He had a big bandage on his kisser," he explained.

Riley grunted. "He was slugged up in the key club," he said.

"Can you describe the clothes he was wearing?" Deglin asked.

"Well, a raincoat, one of them double-breasted ones, dark hat pulled down, and that bandage, like I was saying." He stopped.

"Was he carrying anything?"

Gold slapped his forehead. "A course. Big canvas bag, like the army guys."

No one said anything then and Gold, aware he was finished, got to his feet reluctantly and went to the door.

"This guy done something?" he said to Knight hopefully.

Knight shook his head. "We just want to find him. Thanks a lot."

Gold bobbed his head. "Yes, sir," he said. "Any time."

The door closed after him and Knight said, "Looks like we got him."

"Those night ticket sellers wouldn't be on duty now," Deglin said.

"No," Knight said. "You and Riley want to take it from here?"

Deglin nodded. "Give me those pictures. Is one of them Paine?"

"This one," Knight said and handed him a picture. Deglin looked again at Paine's tanned, good-looking face. And as he looked at the photograph, also in his vision were the knuckles of his right hand, faintly discolored. He shifted the picture to his left.

"Is it a good picture?" he asked after a minute, his voice careful.

Knight shrugged. "Good enough, I guess. The hack driver picked it."

"Who was the other guy he picked?" Deglin said.

"You," Knight said. "An old newspaper picture of you."

Deglin felt his stomach turn. It was an unfamiliar feeling, one he had not had since he was a boy, one he could hardly remember.

"I guess we do look alike."

Knight nodded. "Let me know what you get," he said.

Deglin took the selection of pictures, all except that of himself, and Riley followed him out to a desk. He called the railroads that left Grand Central and talked to the railroad police. After he had told them he wanted to see the ticket sellers who had been on duty at 125th Street after midnight the night before, he had to wait awhile. He hung at the telephone, trying to put from his mind the

NIGHT CRY

growing tightness in his head and throat.

Finally the voice came back on and said that only one had been on duty. "Name's Delsamino, August Delsamino. Lives on a Hundred and Thirty-eighth Street."

Deglin took the address. "He likely home now?" he asked.

"Search me," the voice said. "No phone listed."

"Thanks," he said and hung up. He called Knight's office. "We're going to have to go out on this. We'll use my car."

An hour later, Deglin pulled his convertible up in front of the tall, brownstone tenement not far from his own river-front apartment. But though only a few blocks separated them, their character was as different as though it were miles, or even an era.

Delsamino lived on the fourth floor of the walk-up. When Deglin and Riley entered the imitation marble foyer with its long row of mailboxes and push buttons, there was a murmur throughout the building—a rustle and movement made of a hundred persons living, talking, washing, cooking. Riley rang Delsamino's bell, and after a moment, a door opened on a floor far above. The woman's voice—thin and querulous above the general murmur—came down the stairwell.

Deglin and Riley went half up the first flight.

"Yes?" she called again thinly.

"Is Mr. Delsamino in?" Deglin said.

The tone of her voice altered. "He's asleep. Come back about five."

They continued up the stairs. "We want to see him," Deglin said.

"What do you want?" she said. He saw her head appear over the balustrade. "What is it?" she insisted.

"Police," Riley said heavily.

The noise of the building became a pulsing quiet, as though it had suddenly stopped its normal functions to listen. When they got to the fourth floor, the woman was standing at a doorway. Her face was still, but her eyes were wide.

She opened the door without a word and let them go in ahead of her. "Is there anything wrong?" she asked in a whisper.

"No," Deglin said. "We just have to ask him some questions."

She turned without a sound and disappeared into a back room. Deglin heard her voice, steady though indistinct, then the deeper rumble of Delsamino's, sleepy and discontented. After a moment, he came to the door, trousers pulled over his underwear, his feet thrust in carpet slippers.

"Hello," he said and yawned heavily.

"You were on duty at the Hundred and Twenty-fifth Street station last night," Deglin said.

The man yawned again. He shook his head violently and said, "Yeah. Jesus, I'd just conked off."

"We're looking for a man," Deglin said. "We understand he took a train from your station last night."

Delsamino shrugged. "Lots of guys did," he said.

"Between one and two," Riley said. He had gone to the windows to look out and spoke without turning his head.

"Lots of people don't even buy their tickets there. They got commuter passes and they go right on up to the station," Delsamino said. "We only pay attention if they have to buy a ticket."

"Yes," Deglin agreed. "You might have seen him. He may have been carrying a large army kit bag, and he might have had a white bandage over one eye."

Delsamino scowled and nodded. "Ah," he said. "Snotty fellah."

"You saw him?" Deglin asked.

"One way to Greenwich," Delsamino said. "He practically grabbed the *News* out from under my nose to look at it."

Deglin took the photographs from his pocket and showed him the one of Paine. "Could this be the man?" he asked.

Delsamino turned slightly and held it so the light hit it right. "Yep," he said.

"Thanks for the trouble," Deglin said. Riley came across from the window and they left the apartment.

Downstairs, they chased some kids off the convertible. One said, "Okay, copper," and Deglin knew the word had spread all through the block that they had been there. He drove down to a corner cigar store and parked again. Riley stayed in the car while he called Knight.

"Ticket seller identifies him," he said into the phone. "He bought a one-way to Greenwich."

Knight grunted. "Intends to stay away. He must've seen it."

"That's where this Morgan character is," Deglin said.

"Yeah."

NIGHT CRY 61

"It's a lead," Deglin said.

"It's better than that," Knight said.

"We can go right out now. Call you from there."

"Okay," Knight said. His voice was suddenly troubled. "Talk nice to him, Mark. Don't shy him off."

"I won't," Deglin said, and hung up.

6

When Morgan awoke, the light that filled her room had the watery greyness of dawn, but when she looked at the tiny bedside clock, it was almost noon. She lay quietly, her eyes closed, not wanting to get up, wanting to drift back to sleep.

She gave it a few minutes, but it wouldn't work. Her eyes wouldn't stay closed and her mind wouldn't stay still. It made little pictures for her to view, pictures of Ken's cold anger, of the rainswept, fogbound streets she had walked.

She got out of bed and went into the bathroom. She slid the nightgown off over the smoothness of her body and pinned up her dark hair. Then she turned on the water in the stall shower and stepped under the cool deluge.

It helped. She opened her wardrobe and considered the clothes, deciding that some time on the bridlepath in the whipping wind might help. She dressed quickly and when she had finished went to the long mirror and agreed with herself that the dark jodhpurs and the high-necked sweater and the little hat had helped already.

Downstairs in the kitchen, a big woman in a blue apron was working slowly over the last of an assortment of dishes. When Morgan walked in, she didn't look back over her shoulder, but said distinctly in a warm brogue, "You'll be cooking your own breakfast, young lady."

Morgan said, "Good morning, Mary," and went to the icebox and took out orange juice.

"Gallivantin' till all hours," Mary said.

Morgan looked at the coffee, saw there was enough, and turned on the fire.

"I gallivanted, Mary," she agreed.

"And I suppose young Mr. Paine will be calling the rest of the day trying to piece together where you went," Mary said.

"No danger." She said it in a way that turned the woman from the sink.

NIGHT CRY

"You've had a spat," she charged.

"A dandy, Mary," Morgan said.

"Young people," said Mary, turning back to her work, and it was an indictment.

Morgan drank the orange juice and sipped at her coffee. She watched as the cook put the china away, her eyes following the woman's passage from the sink to the cupboard and back again, though not seeing the familiar pattern of movement.

"There's a bad thing about it," she said finally.

"There's plenty more where he came from," Mary said confidently.

"That's not it. It's that I am probably wrong . . . and he's probably right."

"Then you know what to do," Mary said.

Morgan's head nodded, her eyes still intent and unseeing.

"I did it," she said softly. "I walked around for a long while, and went back to tell him maybe I was wrong. But he was gone."

"He'll be back," the woman said complacently.

"He took his clothes. Almost everything."

The woman started to say something but decided against it. She worked more hurriedly, putting away the last of the dishes.

"Your mother's gone for the afternoon," she said. "Your father drove into New York."

Morgan nodded.

"I've got to go into the Village," Mary said, looking disturbed by her responsibilities.

"All right," Morgan said.

She had another cup of coffee in the silence of the big house before she called a taxi and rode over to the stables.

She let the bay mare have her own way on the bridlepath, and the mare's way was a sedate walk. The clouds in the sky were higher and thinner, though they still moved hurriedly under the urging of the wind. A pale sunshine broke through occasionally, touching the trunks and branches of the huge, shedding trees with a hint of gold.

The mare picked her own paths and when, after a long while, she decided to stop—on a rise that overlooked the rolling hills where autumn revealed houses that had hidden all summer behind the green of the countryside—Morgan again let her have her way.

64 WILLIAM L. STUART

The horse moved under her, straining a little for the brown dry grass along the path, and Morgan leaned forward in the saddle, her arm extended so the mare could eat.

Things were making a little more sense. Perhaps it was because of the wind and the riding, or perhaps it was because there had been time to think about it.

Whether she was deeply in love with Kendall Paine or whether she had once been intrigued by him, an intrigue that had slowly turned to pity as he had changed, she did not know.

But she did know that she had to tell him maybe she was wrong. That would be as much for herself as it would be for him. And if he had moved on the impulse of last night's events, sick of the musty room near the river, finding in it constant reminder of his own failures, he would still be at their restaurant tonight. He had a charge account there. He would have to be.

She jerked the mare's head up from the dried grass and the horse shied quickly in disgust. Morgan wheeled her around and touched her with the crop. The mare broke into an unwilling canter.

Back home, Morgan showered and dressed quickly. Now that she had made up her mind, there was an urgency in her to get the thing done, to see Ken and tell him and let him take it from there. Downstairs again, as she was about to phone for a taxi, the knocker at the front door sounded. She looked again at the commuting schedule, frowned slightly in exasperation, and went to the door.

The two men on the flagged terrace were both big, though the fat one was the taller. She discounted him at once and looked at the other. He was dark, with a handsome intent face. And when he spoke, his voice was polite and at the same time cold and impersonal and commanding.

"Is there a Morgan Taylor here?" he asked.

She nodded her head.

"My name is Deglin," the man said. "I wonder if she might spare us a minute."

She pulled the door a little more closed behind her. "Spare you a minute?" she said.

"I'm sorry," Deglin said. He smiled, and then he laughed. "Are you Miss Taylor? I'm Lieutenant Mark Deglin of the New York Police. This is Detective Daniel Riley." He took a badge from his pocket

NIGHT CRY

and showed it to her. "We can talk out here. It'll only take a minute."

"The police?" Morgan said.

"It's sort of an unofficial visit," Deglin said. "And not at all serious." She smiled back at him, because she had to.

"We wondered if we might talk to Kendall Paine."

She felt the smile go from her face, leaving it stiff and startled. "Talk to him?"

They looked at her pleasantly, not expecting anything. "He hasn't been here," she said.

Deglin smiled again. Riley was still friendly and unperturbed.

"I'll tell you, Miss Taylor," Deglin began, and she liked the easy way he said it. "You were with Mr. Paine last night, and you folks probably missed what happened after you left. There was a homicide at that key club—we already have the person who did it—but we're looking for corroborative statements."

"But we had left," Morgan said, puzzled.

The dark man nodded. "But Mr. Paine had had a fight with the man who was killed."

"Oh," she said.

"You don't know whether he might have gone back to the gambling club after you left? Within the next fifteen minutes? To get something you'd forgotten?"

"No," she said. "I was with him. We didn't go back."

Deglin nodded. "We thought maybe he had," he said pleasantly. "You see, he's gone away, and we thought he might have come up here."

Morgan shook her head. "Why would you think that?"

"When he left, he took a cab to a Hundred and Twenty-fifth Street, and he bought a one-way ticket to Greenwich."

She looked first at Deglin and then at Riley, unbelieving.

They looked back, quietly, interested in her disbelief.

"He didn't come here?" Deglin said.

"No," she said quickly. "Not at all." And at the same time, her heart moved suddenly. Had he come here to tell her that he was wrong? Had he been thinking, there in his room, while she thought?

"Does he know anyone else up here?" Deglin asked.

"A college friend. But he's in California now."

"Does he have any relatives around here?"

"A sister. But she lives near Boston."

"What is her name?" said Riley, his voice rumbling.

"Mrs. John Fleming. Parsonville, Massachusetts."

Deglin took a pad from his pocket and wrote it down.

"Thank you," he said to the girl and smiled. Then he said to Riley, "We can try up there when we get back to the city."

Riley grunted.

The girl stood there, still, looking at Deglin. Abruptly she said, "He could have gone back to New York today. If he came to Greenwich last night he—" she looked for a word, and instantly dropped the search. "He would be back in less than an hour, any time he took the train."

"You think he'll be back there?" Deglin said.

"I'll see him tonight, I'm sure," she said. She looked at them expectantly. "Look," she said. "You're driving back to New York. Will you give me a lift? It's a little restaurant in the Village. You can talk to him."

Deglin looked at Riley, and then nodded to her.

"It'll only take me a minute to get my coat," she said hurriedly. "Thanks."

She turned and let herself in the door and it closed after her.

Riley went back and got into the convertible. When Deglin got in behind the wheel, Riley was looking at him inquiringly.

"There," he said, "is a mixed-up doll."

"They had an argument at the gambling club," Deglin pointed out.

"She didn't believe he'd gone away, but when you told her he definitely had, she didn't argue with it at all," Riley said. "Only she's got a date with him tonight." He wagged his head.

"They had an argument," Deglin said again.

"I guess they did," Riley agreed.

Morgan came out a little later, and the wind whipped her black topcoat around her slim body. Riley got out of the car and held the front seat forward, but when she didn't offer to get into the small seat at the rear, he sighed and squeezed his bulk in.

They said nothing as Deglin took the car out of the drive and turned it toward the Parkway. Deglin glanced at her once, and she was lounging in the corner of the seat, looking ahead, her profile

NIGHT CRY

lovely against the raised collar of the black coat.

"You're pretty sure this fellow is going to meet you?" Riley rumbled after a while.

She nodded and turned in the seat to look back at him. "He will," she said.

"You have a scrap with him?" Riley said conversationally.

"Yes," she said clearly. "But it wasn't a very bad one."

"You like him," Riley said.

"Okay," Deglin said, turning to look back at Riley, and Riley grunted.

She smiled for the first time. "Oh, no," she said, "let's talk."

But Riley had nothing more to say. By the time they had crossed the Harlem River at its juncture with the Hudson, it was completely dark. They moved down the West Side highway, with its rock stitching that keeps the shore from unraveling under the constant wear of the river. At Nineteenth Street, Deglin turned the car down the long narrow ramp to the street. He remembered briefly that Paine waited only a few blocks below, and put the thought from his mind at once.

"Where is this place?" he said.

"On Bleecker Street," she said. "Drive along, and I'll recognize it." She held her wrist out under the dash and leaned forward to look at a small gold watch.

The restaurant was a softly lighted, rambling room that extended at random through the basements of several of the old brownstones. Its ceiling was low and an ancient wooden bar ran across the back of one of the indentations. There were only a few people in the place and Morgan looked at them quickly.

"He'll come to the bar," she said and walked over, Deglin and Riley following her.

She ordered a martini and Deglin asked for Scotch and water. Riley had Irish. They tasted their drinks in silence.

"How long have you known Paine?" Deglin said abruptly.

She turned her head and smiled at him. "Several years. He was convalescing. I was an Army nurse."

He swallowed his drink and pushed some money and his glass across the bar at the bartender.

"Not for me," she said. "This will have to last."

"I'll hold, too," Riley said.

The bartender made Deglin another and he tasted it. "Pretty nice fellow?" he asked.

"He's nice," she said. "Why?"

"I don't know. Just wondered."

"That's odd," she said, laughing. She looked at her watch and half turned on the stool so that she could see the door. "He should be here any minute," she said.

"Sure I can't buy you another?"

She had another martini and Riley had another Irish. And she began to watch the door most of the time. They stopped talking, except for little things that started abruptly and stopped as abruptly. She had nothing to say and apparently Riley could think of nothing.

Finally she finished the martini and got to her feet.

"I'll ask the manager," she said in a troubled way. "He may have phoned."

She was no longer so assured. She went over to the cashier and then to a round little man sitting nearby at a table by himself. They talked for a minute and she came back.

"He called last night, late," she said.

"Yes?" Deglin said.

"He talked to a friend of his."

"No message for you?" Deglin said.

She shook her head. Her teeth were worrying her lower lip.

The door opened, and she turned her face quickly, her eyes lighting. But she turned back again, and said, "I think I'll have another drink."

Deglin put two dollar bills on the bar and nodded to the bartender.

"We're going to have to beat it after this one," he said.

"We'll get someone in that little town you told me about to call on his sister."

"Oh, he'll certainly be here," Morgan objected.

Deglin finished his drink and pushed the change across the bar. Riley got off his stool. "If you hear anything, or if he comes in," he told her, "get in touch with headquarters. They'll get us."

"Yes, Mr. Riley," she said. "Thanks."

Deglin followed Riley out and went around the car to slide behind the wheel. He started the motor, then turned to Riley.

NIGHT CRY 69

"What do you think?" he asked.

"We'd better teletype about the sister. I'll bet he don't show."

Deglin got the notebook from his pocket and gave Riley the name of Paine's sister and the town she lived in.

"What do you think, generally," he urged.

"Christ, we oughta leave them alone," Riley said and chuckled suddenly. "I'll bet he's giving her a slight treatment. Bring her around."

"Maybe," Deglin said seriously.

He pulled the car out from the curb and drove back to the station. They went in together. Knight was still in his office, going through sheaves of reports. He pushed the papers to one side as the men came in and turned his swivel chair as Deglin went over to the window ledge and sat down.

"The guy has good taste in gals," Deglin said.

"She pretty?" Knight said.

"A beaut," Riley said.

Knight grunted with satisfaction. "He'll be back, then," he said.

Deglin looked at Riley and Riley said, "That's what I think. I think we oughta let them alone."

"What do you mean?" Knight said.

Riley grinned. "What's going on there hasn't got anything to do with our problems," he said. "This is just a little of the old absence treatment. Know what I mean?"

Knight grinned too, and so did Deglin.

"I do think we should put a check on the sister," Deglin said.

"Yeah, she's up around Boston," Riley said. "Al, how serious is the DA about finding this guy?"

"He'd like to have him."

"We can get a statement from the girl," Riley said. "She was with him. They didn't go back. Hell, the DA's got enough to fry Carlstrom right now."

Knight shrugged. "You guys'll have to stay on this," he said. "What's the difference, Dan. You'll go down to Twentieth Street and sit on your butt waiting for another homicide anyway. Now you just look for one guy."

"Yeah," Riley said gloomily.

"And as for Mark," Knight looked at Deglin. "You could do

something on a waterfront job starting tomorrow."

"Tomorrow," Deglin said.

Knight nodded.

Deglin went out to a desk and worked out a message for the teletype. He smiled slightly as he hunted out the letters on the typewriter. He found a note that Jane Corby had telephoned him. The same bored woman who had answered the night before came on the phone when he called. She recognized his voice and said, "She's on again, Mr. Deglin. Don't have much luck with her, do you?"

"No," said Deglin, laughing.

"Can she reach you any place?"

"Almost any place," Deglin said, laughing again. "Tell her I'll be moving around the town. Doing a little celebrating."

"Birthday?" the woman said.

"No, no birthday. Just a mild, general celebration."

Deglin dropped in at a place where they had good steaks. Then he went to a nightclub where the bar overlooked the floor, and sat listening to a sad-faced comedian. He found him to be particularly amusing. He left the nightclub following the show, and went to a quiet little bar for a nightcap. It was ordinarily frequented by newspapermen but tonight it was empty. He didn't stay long.

At one in the morning, he opened the door of his apartment and let himself in.

He frowned at a light that burned over one of the easy chairs in front of the fireplace and walked on into the room. Jane Corby lay curled in the chair, her chin cradled in the hollow of her shoulder. He went out and put his coat and hat in the hall closet that was too narrow for the kitbag. Then he came back and took a cigarette from his pocket and lit it.

"Okay, Janie," he said. "Time to get up."

She opened her eyes.

"I wasn't asleep," she said. "I thought you'd be overcome by the sight of my loveliness and helplessness and kiss me."

"I was turned to stone," Deglin said.

She smiled. "Would a drink help, Mark?" She got to her feet and went to the tiny kitchen. She came back with a bottle and two glasses—and Deglin thought, suddenly: I've got to get her out. She

NIGHT CRY

can't see that bag.

She poured some whisky in one glass and handed it to him and then splashed some in her own. "There," she said, smiling.

He drank his down, and then closed his eyes and rubbed the lids slowly. When he opened them and looked at her, she was staring at him with a half-smile. She put her glass down and came over and flung herself at him suddenly.

"Mark," she said in his ear, "am I good for you?"

He wrestled her away a little and she laughed. Her body was full and strong and she pressed it against his. He backed, kissing her neck, until he became shockingly aware that she was backing him toward the bedroom. He pushed her away, and she laughed and cried, "Mark," her head back and her mouth wide with her laughter. She pulled him more strongly and he hit her so hard in the face with his open palm that the impact rang in the apartment.

"God damn it, Jane," he cried. "Stop it."

She stepped back, bent slightly forward, and looked at him her mouth partly open, her face reddening. She ran a hand through her hair, wildly, and looked around.

"Oh," she said. "Oh."

He stood, watching her look frantically around the room, hearing the small sounds that were neither sobs nor breaths but both.

"Jane," he said. "I'm sick. I— I—"

She didn't turn her head toward him again. She found her coat and picked it up by an arm. She left—and she didn't even close the door behind her.

7

The bar had filled until Morgan was pressed from both sides by men and women who talked and laughed and drank, then left for tables and were replaced by others who talked and laughed and drank. Now there were only herself and an elderly man at the other end who circled his glass on the bar and stared into it gloomily.

Morgan finished her fourth martini delicately and put the long-stemmed glass back on the bar. She steadied it as it wobbled and closed her eyes briefly. Her head felt light. It always felt light after only three martinis and now it seemed as though it could easily float away.

She opened her eyes again and turned on the stool toward the door. At first, after Deglin had left, she had been worried. When a half hour had passed with maddening slowness and Paine had not come in, she had been angry and she had rehearsed carefully in her mind the cutting things she would say to him. She had smiled into her third martini at the awkwardness with which he would try to explain his tardiness and the worry that would grow in his eyes during the silent treatment. She would give him the silent treatment, she decided.

And then, as the bartender set the fourth martini before her and it was very late, all that disappeared. And as she drank slowly, sipping to use up the leaden time, the fright returned. She told herself that it was ridiculous to be frightened, that Ken Paine was a man who could take care of himself, and that if a man decided to go away for a while, that was the man's right.

But she didn't believe it. She rose from the stool and walked again through the almost empty restaurant to a table where the fat little manager was reading a tabloid spread out before him. As she came up, he wet his thumb and turned a page.

"I was wondering—" she began.

He looked up and smiled at her.

"It isn't like Mr. Paine," she said.

NIGHT CRY

He nodded.

"He hasn't called?" she asked. "Someone else might have picked up the phone—someone who didn't know I was waiting at the bar." Her eyes were eager.

"No," he said. "I get all the phone calls. They come in right here." He turned in his chair and pointed his fat chin at a phone on the cashier's counter. "I'd a got it," he said.

She smiled. "I guess I'm stood up," she said.

He smiled too and turned back to his paper. Then he lifted his head again. "The feller Mr. Paine called last night is here," he said negligently.

She had started to go, but she stopped. "Where?" she asked.

The fat man pointed his chin again, this time across the room to a table at which two young men were playing checkers. "The big one," he said.

"Oh my gosh," she said joyously. "When did he come?"

"Seems like he's always been here," the fat man said sourly. "But he only came in a little while ago."

The big one was chewing a knuckle and frowning at the board. The little one was leaning back in his chair, his eyes grinning with pleasure over the top of a beer mug. He put the beer mug down and said, as Morgan approached, "There, me hearty."

Morgan looked at the board. The big one was really stuck.

"You've been where you're going," she said.

He looked up and the frown disappeared. Then he got to his feet, shoving the table back against the little man. He got out from behind the table, took her by the arm and guided her gently toward the bar.

"Morgan," he said, "you have a delightfully glassy look through the eyes. My own first love, I think you're ready. Or are you with Ken?"

She smiled at him and nodded.

His face fell. "I'll go back to my checker game," he said, bowing. "I am doing badly, but I will go back. You tell Ken you found me a refreshing and pleasant companion."

"He isn't here," she said.

He lifted his eyebrows. "Well," he said. "Where is he?"

"I don't know," she said. "I thought he'd be here hours ago, Pete.

He hasn't called, and he left no message."

The large young man frowned.

"Did he call you last night, Pete?" she said.

"Will you have a drink?" he asked.

She said no and he had a beer and had a drink of it. Then he scowled at her and said, "I don't understand that. He did call me. He said he was broke, didn't have more than seventy or eighty cents and wanted to borrow twenty. Didn't want to come over here because he was kind of banged up."

"He was in a fight," Morgan said.

"Well, he didn't want to come over," Pete said. "After a while, I went over to his place. It isn't far. But he was gone."

"Did he tell you he was going anyplace?" she asked after a minute. "No."

She considered that carefully.

"Will you have a drink?" he asked.

She shook her head and continued to puzzle. "I don't know," she said finally.

He got another beer and had some of it.

"What don't you know?"

"What got into Ken. He had no money, yet he didn't wait for you to bring some, he just went away. The police think he went away. They know he went away. They thought maybe he came to my house."

"The police?"

She nodded. "I'm frightened, Pete," she said.

He gazed intently at the bottles back of the bar, shook his head, and finally grinned.

"Too much for me," he admitted.

"But he must have borrowed money from someone," she said suddenly. "He must have seen someone before he left."

"Not me," Pete said sharply.

She looked at him. He was withdrawn—not wary, but with no desire to know more about it. The mention of police....

"No, Pete," she said. "Not you."

Then she got her coat and went carefully to the door and found a cab and went to a hotel.

NIGHT CRY

75

8

Deglin was slumped in the chair in front of the fireplace, where Jane had feigned sleep, his hands between his knees. He had stared into the black, dead grate until his eyes ached. He couldn't think about anything. It was as though his brain had become numb. When he tried to consider what else he might have done, to wonder if perhaps he should have just let her go into the bedroom, it was as though his thoughts were eyes entering a black room.

Nor could he understand his despair. No one knew, he told himself. No one would learn. The police were washing it out. He had only to get rid of the kitbag. A cab driver and a ticket seller were sworn to the fact that they had seen Paine. There was still a train conductor, if his word were needed.

It came back.

The train was not crowded. It was easy to find a seat on the right side of one of the cars, and to put the bag on the seat beside him, stenciled name to the aisle, to discourage anyone from sitting down and possibly making conversation.

The rain scarred the windows so that it was practically impossible to see out, but he wiped away a misted section and watched the distorted lights of the Harlem River as the train crossed over it.

The conductor moved through the train just after they had entered the Bronx. He handed the conductor his ticket and the man put it in his pocket, then punched a long stub and put it in the band of Deglin's hat for him.

"Have you a commuter's schedule?" Deglin asked.

The conductor looked at him, fumbled in his pocket and finally pulled one out and handed it over.

"Is my watch right?" he asked then. "Damn near missed this."

The conductor fished out his big railroad watch. "One thirteen."

"Thanks," and the conductor went up the aisle, glancing first to the right and then to the left at the stubs in the seats.

He watched the conductor go, then he looked at his watch and set it. It had been two minutes slow and he wanted it right. Then he looked at the schedule. The next stop was at 1:42. He wondered how long it would take him to change his clothes, and he figured five minutes. He waited, looking at his watch often. When it said 1:35, he got to his feet and started up the aisle, carrying his bag. At the end of the car, he tried the door of the men's room. He pushed it heavily.

It was locked.

He went through the next car more quickly, bouncing the heavy bag against the seats with the swaying of the train. The next men's room was locked, too. He tried it only once, and then pushed open the door into the next car. He glanced quickly down the length of the car, and the conductor was sitting halfway down, going carefully through his stubs, making notations on a sheet of paper. He tried the door of the ladies' room. It opened, and he stepped in. He looked at his watch and he had only four minutes.

He ripped the straps from the bag and opened it. He took the eye patch off his eye and stripped off the raincoat and jacket and trousers. He started to pull the necktie down and looked at his watch. He wouldn't have time, he decided, and pulled the tie back up. He was fumbling feverishly with the straps of the bag, trying to get them back, when the train began to slow to a stop. He finally got the second buckled, set his own hat on his head, snicked the lock back, and stepped out. A sleepy looking couple glanced at him as he joined them on the platform. The train reached a full stop and they got off into the driving rain.

And that was it . . . excepting the crowd that kept him from doing anything with the bag . . . youngsters, lively and laughing, who were waiting for the train to New York. He waited with them . . . Then the cab to his own apartment. That was it . . . that was all of it . . . that was....

The andirons in the fireplace gleamed, reflecting the light from the lamp at his side.

That was it, except that Paine had not stopped living like those thousands of others who were dead. He was beginning to become alive. The others had never been more than dead men and women—but Paine was beginning to live, through the sighing of a lovely blonde woman.

NIGHT CRY

Deglin tried once again, desperately, to find a place in the apartment for the kitbag. And after he had lain in bed for a long time, sleepless, he got up and tried all the same places all over again. The bag sat in his bedroom the rest of the night, Paine's name against the wall, but visible just the same as Deglin stared up into the darkness.

9

Deglin rid himself of the kitbag the next morning. First, he called the station and left a message that he'd be late. Then he called a storage company in the Chelsea district, picking it at random from the classified telephone book, and asked them to send up a truck for a package to be stored.

By the time the truck arrived, he had secured a large cardboard box from storage downstairs and filled it with the kitbag, some clothes of his own of which he had tired, and a few old books.

The two men who came for the pickup looked at the roped box with pleasure, and while the smaller began wrestling it toward the door, the larger laboriously made out a receipt, frowning over his pad and wetting the stub of a pencil with his tongue. When he wrote down Deglin's name, he said, "You're the detective, ain't you?"

Deglin said he was.

"Ain't got any dead bodies in there, have you?" the large man said, grinning.

Deglin grinned back at him. "No, not this trip," he said.

"Well, by God, we've had them down at the place, Mr. Deglin," the large man said. Then he yelled, "Ain't we, Joe?"

Joe, who had moved the case to the foyer, stuck his head around the door. "Got what?" he said.

"Remember that stiff we stored couple years ago?"

Joe nodded, said, "It began to stink," without any particular emotion, and disappeared again.

"You didn't work on that case," the large man said, handing Deglin the receipt. "When you want this again, just refer to this number. Better not lose it."

"I won't," Deglin said, "Thanks."

The men left, their voices rumbling in the foyer as they gave one another instructions. Deglin folded the receipt. He looked at the desk, decided against putting the receipt there, and slid it into his wallet.

NIGHT CRY

That was it. In a year or so, when Paine had been forgotten—when he had become only a fleeting remembrance that once in a while stopped Morgan Taylor at what she was doing and caused her to stare unseeing into space, when he had become a part of the police filing system and little more—then something could be done about the kitbag.

He got to the station a half-hour later. Riley was laying out a game of solitaire, and when he saw Deglin, he inclined his head toward Knight's office, scraped the cards together, and dropped them in a drawer.

Knight looked as though he had slept well. He was back in his swivel chair, which he had swung around toward the window, and he had his finger tips together. He was finishing up something as Deglin and Riley walked in, and the young cop seated at the other side of the desk was listening and nodding.

"Just keep your eyes open," Knight said, and the young cop got to his feet.

Riley beat Deglin to the window and half-sat against the ledge. Deglin waited until the young cop had picked some papers off Knight's cluttered desk, then he sat in the chair just vacated. Knight swung his chair around, opened a drawer and took out a sheet of paper. He looked at it for a moment, then put it on the desk with the rest of the litter.

"We haven't got anything yet from that little town in Massachusetts," he said.

"They probably haven't had time to check," Deglin said. "Probably had to phone the teletype from Boston."

"I think this went to the State police," Knight said. "They got stations everyplace." He picked up the sheet of paper from his desk. "In the meanwhile, I've told the DA's office about what the girl says." He waved the paper. "The DA says he wants us to run down this kid just on the chance the girl is covering the fact he saw Morrison get it."

"Oh, Jesus," Riley said, shaking his head.

"Can I help it?" Knight demanded. "He don't want to go in front of a jury until he's got an airtight case—says he's sick of going up with some confessed killer and then have him plead duress and police brutality and get away with it."

"That wasn't brutality," Riley said, "I only shot him."

"That's what the DA says," Knight grunted and looked at Deglin. "Stop grinning," he added.

"Well, I don't see any sense of chasing that dame," Riley began. "She was expecting him last night—looked pretty unhappy because he wasn't showing, and—"

"Okay, okay," Knight said. "I'm only telling you we gotta keep an eye on it. I've given it to Missing Persons and they're following through, but we just gotta keep an eye on it. And Dan, you're to be attached to the case from Homicide until he turns up."

Riley nodded and looked out the window.

"You've written it up, what you've done?"

"This morning," Riley said.

Knight nodded. "I can send that up to him. It oughta shut him up for a while. In the meantime, Mark, there's this waterfront stuff I was talking about."

Deglin nodded.

Knight found another folder and was going through it. "You can study it, but in brief it's like this. You'll work with Klein. He can do most of it. It's not in our district, but we've been called in anyway. More and more stuff is disappearing outa lofts and those waterfront sheds over on the West Side. It's getting into circulation some way or another and it's damn valuable stuff. The shipping companies are raising hell with the mayor and he's giving it to the commissioner and he's giving it to the department. Maybe some of your stools can help."

Deglin took the folder and started looking at the typewritten reports. "Any lead on the fence?" he asked.

Knight shook his heavy head. "No leads on nothing," he said. "That's why we want you guys on it."

Deglin got to his feet. "I'll get Klein. We'll report in later," he said.

"And I'll let you know if we get anything from Massachusetts," Knight said.

Riley followed Deglin out the door. "Brother," he said. "The DA must really be eating at Al's tail."

Deglin grinned, "It's a job I've decided I wouldn't have," he said.

"By God," Riley said, looking at him. "You do look better like you got something off your chest."

NIGHT CRY

Deglin thought briefly of the kitbag. "I feel better," he said, and he sounded as though he did.

He found Klein downstairs talking to the desk sergeant. They looked over the folder together, making notes. When they had finished, they went around the corner for coffee. Riley was already there. The waiter set coffee in front of them and Deglin stirred his while Klein examined the row of pies at the back of the counter and decided on a wedge of apple.

"Seems to me I've heard that the Scalise boys have been showing some big dough around lately," Deglin said, as the waiter slid the pie onto a plate and set it in front of Klein.

Klein conveyed a large forkful to his mouth and chewed. He swallowed and nodded. "Been thinking of that," he said.

"Want to nose around a little?" Deglin asked. "I can put out some feelers of my own."

Riley finished his coffee and set the heavy cup down. "Here comes the yellow press," he said.

Deglin turned and nodded to Clement Smith, who slid his legs over a stool and began an immediate inspection of the pie racks.

"You were going to keep me filled in," he said to Deglin, and squinted at a freshly cut blueberry pie.

Deglin tried his coffee. "Nothing's cooking," he said. "It's like you heard." He turned to look at the newspaperman, and Smith was still regarding the blueberry pie, his lean, bored face thoughtful.

The waiter moved up along the counter and Smith pointed at the pie. "One of those, a big one," he said, "and slap on a big ball of the vanilla."

"Hello, Mr. Smith," the waiter said.

Smith grinned at him. "A cup of your poisonous coffee too," he said; and then, as the waiter moved quickly away he added for Deglin: "I've been talking to the DA's office."

Deglin finished his coffee. "Yes," he said.

Smith nodded. "He isn't pulling the plug on Carlstrom until you turn up this guy Paine. So you missed him the other night?"

"He'd gone some place," Deglin said.

Smith nodded. The waiter brought the pie and ice cream and slid it across the marble counter. Smith turned it slowly in front of him and began to pat the ice cream down with his fork. Deglin watched, his eyes smiling.

"Why aren't you over at Paddy's getting bagged with the rest of the boys?" he said.

Riley leaned over in front of Deglin. "Yeah," he said—and laughed. "You ain't seen pie and ice cream since you learned that fruit juice ferments."

Smith turned and grinned engagingly. "Okay," he said. "But news is kind of thin."

"What's the matter with the dames over in domestic relations court?" Riley demanded. "You can always get a good dirty story out of them."

Smith ignored his ice cream and it began to melt, mixing the blue of the pie with its own whiteness. "There's a dame in the Paine thing," he said.

"Yeah," Riley said. "But for Christ's sake don't you start mixing it up."

Deglin looked at Smith.

"The kid's gone," Smith said. "The DA is waiting for him. The girl's name is Morgan Taylor."

"Riley's right," Deglin said carefully. "She and the kid had a fight. He isn't mixed up in the murder anyway. Let it be."

Smith spooned up a bit of the ice cream. "They'd been playing around in a pretty fancy gambling joint," he said. "The kid's wanted. Seems to me—"

"We've dropped that," Deglin said quickly. "Klein and I are on something a hell of a lot more interesting."

Smith turned on his stool and looked at Riley. "Then what are you still doing around?"

"He's lazy," Deglin said. "He also wants a lesson in how we crack this waterfront stuff."

"Got anything?" Smith asked.

"Not yet," Deglin said. "Tonight maybe."

Smith nodded. "That might be something," he said. But he did not seem interested in it. He toyed with his pie and ice cream for a while longer, drank his coffee, said something vehement about Notre Dame's chances in the football game of the weekend, then left. Riley watched him stalk out. "Paddy's in five minutes," he said with some amusement.

NIGHT CRY

83

"I don't know," Deglin said. "He's after something. He wants a story."

Riley finished a second cup of coffee and left. Klein left at the same time. Deglin spent a little longer with his second cup and finally paid his check and left too.

He went, apparently without any specific plan, to a number of unrelated places. He stopped in a cigar store on Eighth Avenue in the Fifties and talked prize fights with the man behind the counter. The man behind the counter was known as German Louie and it was known that, if he did not himself put bets down, he could always get a bet put down, whether it was for fifty cents or fifty thousand.

"Does that Ruffy-Larkin thing look right to you at eight to five?" Deglin said, after he had bought a package of cigarettes and had lit one.

German Louie shrugged. "To me," he said, "they're all wrong, and you know it."

Deglin nodded. "I'm thinking of sending a C note looking for company," he said. "Any of the smart boys giving indications?"

German Louie's eyes were masked. "Couple of the brothers seem to like Ruffy," he said.

"At eight to five," Deglin said and lifted his eyebrows. German Louie shrugged. "Maybe they like him so much they'd like him at eighty to five."

"That's liking," Deglin said. "Mannie Scalise sometimes knows."

"Did I say Mannie?" German Louie demanded.

"You didn't say it wasn't Mannie," Deglin pointed out. "I hadn't known he was spending heavy."

"I didn't say anything," German Louie said, and went to the other end of the counter.

Deglin took a cab from there to a saloon on Second Avenue in the Sixties. He went into the bar and leaned against one end of the mahogany and ordered a Scotch. Only the bartender talked to him, and then only to take his order. But when Deglin left, he said that he would probably drop in much later that night and he left a good tip.

He talked to a cab driver who was a friend of his and complained only about the nasty weather. Deglin didn't seem to ask him much of anything and the cab driver didn't seem to tell him much of anything—except that he did say he had heard, in a roundabout way he couldn't check, that a store in the Bronx seemed to have some pretty good bargains in imported fabrics and perfumes.

"Took a couple of grifters up there," the cabbie said.

"Out of the way place, wouldn't you say?" Deglin asked.

The cabbie nodded. "Damndest thing how they get wind of those places," he said and drove off.

Deglin returned to the station in the middle of the afternoon. Klein was already there, hunched over the folder of reports. As Deglin came in, he was wetting a thumb preparatory to turning a page, but he looked up and leaned back in the chair instead.

"That Scalise hunch looks like a good one," he said.

Deglin sat down and pushed his hat to the back of his head.

"Tenuous," he said. "Getting someone to talk is going to be a problem."

"I've put a few lines out," Klein said. "May pick up something tonight."

"Have you got a list of important warehouse holdings?"

Klein shook his head and made a note. "I'll get that," he said. "I figured whoever is knocking these places off is probably doing it from the inside."

Deglin nodded. "Then we'll put a check on the night men in every damn warehouse carrying valuable shipments. I've put out lines for some of the boys who know the talk around—" He stopped, because Klein was looking at the door behind him with some interest, and turned his head. Then he took his feet from the desk and got out of the chair.

"Hello," he said—and his voice was flat.

Morgan Taylor stood behind the short railing with Clement Smith. Her face was grave and troubled. Smith was smiling slyly.

"You went out to see her," Deglin said.

Smith nodded. "Glad I did," he said, still smiling.

"Hello, Mr. Deglin," she said. She looked at Klein and didn't know him, so she said nothing more.

Deglin moved over and half sat against the desk, indicating with a slight nod the chair he had vacated. She sat in it, her gloved hands in her lap.

NIGHT CRY

"You—you haven't had any word yet?" she asked softly.

Deglin shook his head.

"I've got something that might be interesting," Smith said from the doorway.

Deglin looked at him. "What's that?" he asked.

"Paine saw someone last night none of us knows about."

"Look," said Deglin. "Why are you making this a big thing? The kid's gone away for a while. We'll turn him up."

"Still, he saw someone last night that you don't know about. Neither does Miss Taylor," Smith said. "She'd like to find him."

"What makes you think he saw somebody?" Deglin said.

"He had to," Smith said. "He called a guy named Pete Redfield. Wanted to borrow twenty because he was flat. When Redfield got over to his place, though, he had already gone."

Deglin grunted. "He paid a cab bill—a big one—and bought a ticket."

"That's what I said," Smith pointed out, and leaned against the doorway.

Deglin kept his eyes on the girl. She looked a little strained and confused.

"You know what Smith wants to do," he said to her.

She shook her head.

"He wants to turn the *Globe* loose on you. It's got all the angles for a juicy *Globe* story."

She looked quickly at Smith and Smith smiled again.

"I'd tell him to go to hell," Deglin said.

"The DA wants to talk to Paine," Smith said to Morgan Taylor. "We'll find him for you. For God's sake, he's no crook. We handle it right, he sees that his girl is worried and he can straighten things out just by showing himself and bingo—there he is."

Deglin didn't look at him. He watched Morgan Taylor. The muscle jumped suddenly in his jaw, and he stood away from the desk, and walked casually to the window and looked out. He said to himself that for Christ's sake it didn't mean anything but he should stop it right now.

He said, casually, without turning his head from the window, "We'll turn him up, without all the publicity."

She was hesitant and he turned to see her frowning at him.

"But it does seem so much quicker—" she began.

Deglin came back from the window. "You may want a gang of subway riders giggling over your troubles," he said harshly. "You may even be pleased with the thought of a lot of degenerates looking at your picture and estimating the enjoyment you provided Paine." He stopped because she looked startled. "You've *read* the *Globe*, haven't you?" he demanded.

Morgan nodded.

"I hadn't planned to handle it that way," Smith said.

"However you handle it," Deglin said, "it's publicity, and lots of it. *We'll* find Paine."

"So will we," Smith said easily. "Quicker."

Deglin ignored him. "Look," he said to Morgan Taylor, "would you like to see how we operate in looking for people? Maybe that'll convince you."

She was pleased. She smiled and her eyes brightened. "It would be helpful," she said.

Deglin looked at Klein. "You'll get after that stuff we were talking about?" he asked and Klein nodded. "And if Dan comes in, tell him I'll be downtown, at Centre Street."

Smith stepped aside to let Deglin and Morgan pass him in the doorway; then he grinned briefly at Klein, who scowled.

Smith turned to follow them.

10

The elevator stopped on the fifth floor of the somber grey building in Manhattan's roaring lower East Side, and they stepped out into a plain reception room separated from the main corridor of the floor by wide steel mesh.

Deglin said, "Excuse me a minute," and went through an open doorway in the mesh, past a shirt sleeved officer with a telephone operator's headset hanging loosely around his neck, and turned down the corridor. There was a subdued air of activity, an undercurrent of motion and sound that was shattered once by a muffled metallic howl that brought to them an unintelligible, bigger-than-life voice.

Smith grinned at Morgan. "We're going to see the Telegraph Bureau. And that's probably the two-way marine radio," he explained. "It really pounds in."

She nodded, still a little startled, as the sound cut off abruptly.

Deglin came back then and waited for them inside the corridor. They followed him down the hall to a frosted-glass door. The room they entered was long and L-shaped, with a smaller, glass-fronted room forming the inner section of the L. Down one wall was a string of telephone switchboards, where a row of men and women worked steadily at the beckoning of the winking lights, their voices a monotonous undertone. In the middle of the room, at a smaller bank of boards, policemen worked, their voices heavier, sometimes urgent.

"This is bigger than any newspaper," Deglin said.

She nodded, watching the quick movements of the men slowly make a pattern in the confusion.

"They're in touch with everyone all the time," Deglin said at her side. "All the time. Hospitals, morgue, district attorney, fire department, medical examiner, railroads, airports."

"A lot of nickels," Smith said.

"A lot of nickels," Deglin agreed. He took Morgan's elbow and led her down the aisle between the telephone boards to a quieter room that opened off the L. There, a grey-haired, blue-eyed man, standing in the middle of an enormous U-shaped table, looked up and smiled.

"Hello, Mark," he said.

"Hello, Captain," Deglin said.

A young, shirt-sleeved officer came from a microphone beyond the table and handed the grey-haired man a slip of paper. He leaned over the table, checked the slip and wrote down three numbers on it. The young man went back to the microphone and his voice came to them cryptically.

"Look at it," Deglin said. "It's New York."

She went to the huge table, smiling at the grey-haired man who smiled back. On the table, in front of him, and at his sides, lay the outlines of New York—of Manhattan, Queens, Brooklyn, Staten Island and the Bronx—each with its streets carefully marked, each interlined with colors. And on a glass pane extending over the entire table rode hundreds of numbered counters.

She turned to Deglin. "It looks awfully involved," she said.

"It's terribly simple," he said. "That man is at most a minute from anywhere in greater New York."

"A minute?"

"About. Those counters are the police department patrol cars and the detective cruise cars. When something happens, anything the police department is interested in, the Telegraph Bureau is called on that switchboard over there. The captain here locates the trouble and dispatches the nearest patrol cars and cruise car. He's only an instant from them, and they're only a minute from any point in the city. The police department works like a cat catching a mouse. Or a dog catching a cat. We wait for them to run. When they run, we've got them."

She went to the table once more and returned. "They know about Ken?"

"They know about him," Deglin said. "Every one of them. They know what he looks like, how he dresses, where he was last seen."

"What he looks like?"

Deglin nodded. "Enough. If they see anyone who looks like him, they'll question him."

"And if it isn't Ken?"

NIGHT CRY   89

Deglin smiled. "Then they'll let him go. If it was really a big hunt, the print shop would do pictures of him, then they'd really know."

"But that," she said, looking at the table again, "is only New York City. He got on a train."

Deglin nodded and turned back into the big L-shaped room. The glass-fronted room that was a part of it, and yet apart from it, held rows of teletype machines. Two of them were clattering vigorously, and over their noise Deglin said, "We're only a minute or two from the whole Northeast, and not much more than that from the rest of the world."

He went to one of the machines and held up the long paper covered with messages. For a moment he looked at it, then he said, "Look at this."

She could understand the part that said Kendall Paine, but the rest was beyond her.

"What does it say?" she asked.

"Paine did not go to his sister's," Deglin said, looking at the message again. "She had a letter from him this morning, and in it he said something about having to get away to think some things out."

He looked at her and saw that she was frowning and relieved at the same time. Then he ran he paper through his hands and stopped at another message. "The Greenwich police will check the hotels," he said.

She didn't pay any attention to that.

"Why," she said, "that means that he's probably back in town right now." She turned to Smith. "If we go to the Bleecker Street restaurant, he may be there."

Smith nodded.

"You're having dinner together?" Deglin said.

"Mr. Smith was going to buy me cocktails."

"Would you like to see more down here?"

"More?" she asked.

"Missing Persons? The Lab? The Print Shop?"

"But he must be back in town," Morgan repeated. And then, she added, as though she had suddenly remembered her manners, "This is really tremendously interesting, Mr. Deglin."

Deglin went with them. Smith didn't like the idea, but he grinned engagingly enough when Deglin suggested suddenly that he'd come along in case Paine had shown up. Morgan was pleased. She said, "Oh, he'll certainly be there tonight. Why"—and her relief was evident—"I'll bet he's already called me at home."

Deglin smiled. "So there's nothing to get steamed up about—and Clem here is out of a story."

Smith nodded. "Maybe. Anyhow, I can still do a follow-up," he said.

They took a cab up and across to the small restaurant, and when they walked in the door, Morgan was smiling. She nodded brightly at the round little man behind the cash register.

"Has Mr. Paine been in?" she asked.

"Nope," he said. He'd had an early dinner. He was exploring his teeth carefully with a toothpick. "The other guy is here," he said.

Morgan nodded, and Deglin and Smith followed her through one of the connected rooms to where Pete Redfield slouched on a bench against the wall, reading an evening paper and moving an empty glass back and forth on the wooden top of the table in front of him.

She stopped and said, "Hello, Pete."

He put the paper down and looked up at her. "Hello, Morgan," he said, and started to smile until he saw Deglin and Smith behind her. Then he pushed the table forward and got to his feet and looked at them seriously. He loomed above both Deglin and Smith, so that he inclined his head slightly to look at them.

"This is Mr. Smith, a newspaperman," Morgan said, and Redfield looked at both of them until Smith put out his hand. "And Mr. Deglin, a detective," she added.

Redfield looked at Deglin with interest. "I've heard of you," he said.

"Not always a good idea for a detective," Smith said, looking at Deglin. "But Mark here makes it work. Sometimes I think the majority of the catches he makes are pre-caught by his publicity. They hear Deglin's on the case, shrug and say, 'What's the use. Might as well give up.'"

"You do get a lot of them, don't you?" Redfield said.

"A share," Deglin said.

Redfield looked back at the table and said suddenly, "Why don't

NIGHT CRY

you sit down? Have a drink?"

"Thanks, Pete," Morgan said, and slid in behind the table. Redfield waited until Smith had moved in beside her. He and Deglin sat on the outside.

They didn't say anything for a minute, except to order drinks. Then Redfield looked curiously across at Morgan, and she said:

"We thought Ken might drop in."

Redfield lifted heavy, light eyebrows. "Hasn't he shown yet?"

"But he didn't go to his sister's," Morgan said. "He really should drop in here tonight."

Redfield looked at Smith and Deglin and grinned. "He must know where the crown jewels are," he said.

Morgan frowned. "It—" she began; then she laughed and looked at Deglin. "It does seem kind of silly," she said. "After all, he is a grown man."

Deglin nodded. "That is exactly what I mean," he said. "Now if you can only point that out to our friend Smith."

Smith nodded and smiled.

"I looked up the stuff in the morgue on him," he said, easily. "Quite a guy. Your name was mentioned, Redfield."

"We played football," Redfield said.

"You also whacked him in the eye. Six months ago? Outside El Morocco?" Smith smiled.

Pete Redfield scowled. "That was a lot of crap," he said. He looked at Morgan and flushed deeply. "He was just a little out of line. It wasn't important at all."

Smith ignored it. "Fine football player, isn't he?" he asked.

Redfield nodded. "One of the greatest. More drive than any back I ever saw in action. Did a good job in the war, too. Same kind of job. Didn't care about anything."

"I found a copy of his citation," Smith said in his negligent way. "Something wrong with his head?"

Morgan looked shocked. "He was in the hospital for a long while," she said sharply. "He was hit by shrapnel."

"They had to do something to his head," Smith said. "I called the Vet Administration."

Deglin looked at him. Smith had done a lot of things while he wasn't over at Paddy's.

"He won't thank you for all this nosing around," Deglin said.

Smith smiled quietly. "He'll be in in a minute. Then he won't have to thank me."

They talked for a while longer—about football and this and that—and Deglin heard Smith carefully drop a question now and again about Paine. Out of it, Deglin knew, Smith was making his story. Nor was there much he would be able to do about it. Smith was like that. He did his stories and he ran them as he saw fit. Deglin had used him at times, but only when it met the convenience of each of them. And he knew that he himself had been used.

After an hour, Pete Redfield left. He had planned to eat there, but he left anyway, embarrassed by the way the conversation returned at intervals to Paine and by Smith's casual but pointed inquiries on each of those opportunities. Before he left, he had had a chance to talk to Deglin. Deglin had left the table to go to the toilet, and Redfield followed him almost at once. While Deglin was washing his hands, Redfield stood at the mirror, crouching a little so that he could see to comb his hair.

"That newspaper guy is a snotty fellow," he said tentatively, looking into the mirror.

"Good newspaperman," Deglin said.

"It'd probably be outa line to smack him one," Redfield said.

"It would be a good way to get even a worse story than what he'll probably run," Deglin said. "Was Morgan your girl before Paine came along?"

Redfield straightened and looked at him. He was big.

"Why?" he said.

"That's what Smith thinks," Deglin said, and opened the door and went out.

Redfield left shortly after that, pleading a dinner date uptown. Morgan, who had become uncertain about Paine's appearance in the restaurant, regretted seeing him go. She had had three martinis, each held long after it had become warm, and she looked as though she were not particularly enjoying herself. Smith seemed impatient to get going. After a period of little conversation, he got to his feet and put a bill on the table.

"Take care of mine, Mark?" he asked.

Deglin pushed it back to him. "It's on me," he said.

NIGHT CRY

"Thanks," Smith said, and put the bill back in his pocket. "I've really got to get going," he said to Morgan.

She smiled, but she obviously didn't know exactly what to say.

"I'll see you again," Smith said.

She nodded and said, "Of course."

Deglin got to his feet and, when she looked momentarily concerned, smiled and told her he would be right back. Then he walked with Smith through the emptying restaurant to the door. It was colder in the street and the wind had risen again. It whipped at Smith's topcoat and he had to hold onto the brim of his hat as he waited for Deglin to speak.

Deglin said nothing for a moment. He looked down the dimly lit street and wondered how he could stop Smith from running the story. He didn't want it run. He hadn't counted on it—and though, for the moment, he could not project its effects, he had a feeling that the story was against him.

"I know what you're going to ask me," Smith said finally.

Deglin turned his head to him. "I don't want that story run."

Smith shrugged. "Looks like a good story."

"Paine may still turn up. Good God, man, if he does, tonight, and you run it, you're going to look like a jerk."

"You don't know Smith," Smith said. Then, suddenly, there was a glint of amusement in his voice as he added, "This is the first time I've known you to be concerned about a story, Mark."

"What do you mean?"

"A very attractive girl," Smith said, and turned and walked off into the night.

When Deglin returned to the table, Morgan looked as though she had resolved something. The faint strain that showed in her face had lessened, though it had not entirely disappeared. Her grey eyes seemed brighter.

Deglin sat opposite her and she looked at him and smiled.

"Are you going to take me to dinner, Mr. Deglin?" she asked.

He nodded. "Anywhere," he said.

"Not here," she said decisively. She half-turned on the bench to pull her topcoat over her slim shoulders, then waited for him to pull the table out.

"You haven't given up," Deglin said.

She sat back and looked at him levelly. "You'll think me a schoolgirl. You've probably thought me one already," she said. "But it has just occurred to me that I must look like an awful dope sitting around mooning over a guy who doesn't even think enough of me to call up and tell me not to worry about him."

"He's had something on his mind," Deglin pointed out.

She nodded. "Well, it isn't me," she said. "So I'm getting him off mine."

Deglin pulled the table forward and, when she had slid out, paid the check and followed her to the door.

They went to midtown on the East Side, to a tiny steak place he knew. They had martinis and this time Morgan did not let them stand until they had become warm. Deglin found himself fascinated with her, and with the change in her. She had a way of leaning forward when she listened, her red lips slightly parted, her grey eyes intent and questioning—and when she laughed, her eyes lighted suddenly and she tossed her dark head back.

The Swiss who ran the place finally came to their table around eleven o'clock and said apologetically that he'd like to close.

"People don't understand, Mr. Deglin," he said. "We restaurant people, we're up again at five in the morning, down at the market."

"S'all right," Deglin said.

"Oh," Morgan said. "Playing the market. No wonder you have to run a restaurant, too."

And while Deglin paid the check, the proprietor explained carefully exactly what he meant by the market and she listened in her intent way.

They went to a small club that was raucous with music. The headwaiter put them at a small table against the wall, so that they sat pressed together. It was too loud for talk. They drank their drinks and when Deglin occasionally looked at Morgan, she was watching the five-piece band up on the stand, her profile pale in the half-darkness. She liked the savagery of the music; her warm thigh, pressed against his, moved with its rhythm.

Just before one, when the blaring of the horns, and the insistent throbbing of the bass and the drums had stopped for a moment, Deglin looked at his watch.

"I'm sorry," he said. "There is something I have to do."

NIGHT CRY

She was incredulous.

"Now?" she asked. "What would you do now?"

"Make a living," he said.

She was contrite. "I'd forgotten," she said. "You've been awfully nice and this has been a wonderful time."

"I've liked it," Deglin said.

Her train left Grand Central shortly after one, and they got there with a few minutes to spare. She stood outside the entrance of the last car and talked for a minute about the band they had heard. Late commuters, hurrying for the train, slowed enough so that they could look at her as they passed. When she went in, she sat on the side on which Deglin stood and put her face up against the window. Deglin walked down the length of the car to where she was, smiled at her, and waved before he turned and went out of the station.

He thought of her in the cab going to the bar up on Second Avenue. They were not active thoughts but she remained on his mind. It was a part of this thing that had happened, he told himself. She was a warmness in his mind, and there was no strain or worry or memory. It occurred to him, as the cab moved across town in the Fifties, that he could not remember the events of two nights before— at least, not as though they had happened to him. Some things he could remember, but they were only bits and pieces. The girl who had smiled at the car cards on the subway and had looked at him with interest. He remembered her. The gambler's murderous look when he'd taken the address book from his pocket. The hissing of the bubbles in the dark waters of the slip, like the bubbles in a glass of charged water—no, that was wrong, there had been the howl of the wind, and the lonesome hoot of the fog horns, and one other thing. Whistling? Yes, soundless almost even to himself. His own tuneless whistling under the exertion of his breathing. Completely without tune, for he could not remember the song. And one other thing he remembered: Jane Corby's gasping, crying sob. The muscle in his jaw twitched. But all else—those things that keep men awake—had washed out with the departure of the kitbag that morning.

He paid the cab in front of the saloon and walked in. It was the same he had visited earlier in the afternoon. Now, it was warmly lighted, pleasant with the quiet talk of a group of men at the bar. Two voices rose above the rest and Deglin identified them quickly as elderly men who spent their nights in loud and amiable argument.

Deglin took a table in the back and the bartender came across with a double Scotch and set it down. He ran his cloth over the whitened wood of the top and said, "Anything else, Mr. Deglin?"

"Anyone in?" Deglin asked.

The bartender nodded.

"Thanks," Deglin said, and took some papers from his pocket.

He sat for the space of twenty minutes, studying the jotted notes on the waterfront robberies and the Scalise brothers. Occasionally, he underlined something, but mostly he read over and over. When, finally, the chair opposite him was pulled out and the voice said, "Hiya," he merely looked up, nodded and put the notes back in his pocket again.

The man who had joined him sat not quite looking at him. He was thin, with a long ugly face, a slash of a mouth that wore a perpetual sneer, and light protruding eyes that moved constantly. In the softly golden light of the saloon, they flashed whitely, and Deglin waited until they rested momentarily on him before he spoke.

"How're things, Izzie?" he asked.

"Slow. Slow," Izzie said, his eyes shifting away and back again.

"Buy you a drink?"

"Could use one. Use a million," Izzie said.

Deglin lifted his hand to the bartender, who came around the end of the bar to their table.

"Bring Izzie here a double," Deglin told him. "And bring me another, too."

The bartender nodded and went away. They said nothing more until he had returned with the drinks, made another pass at the table with the bar rag, and returned behind the bar. Izzie drank deeply, his eyes steady over the rim of the glass.

"You been being a good boy?" Deglin said.

The slash in Izzie's face opened in what was meant to be a grin.

"I gotta, chief. Gotta," he said.

"How you making a living, Izzie?"

NIGHT CRY

Izzie shook his head slowly. "Little here. Little there. All on the square, chief. All on the square."

"I'm curious about some things," Deglin said.

Izzie's eyes moved suddenly, quickly, toward the door and the bar and the tables.

"It's no rap on you," Deglin said slowly. "Another drink?"

He went to the bar and picked up the double for Izzie and brought it back and set it down. While Izzie drank it, he watched him. Izzie was the true criminal. He was the underworld of the city. His stuttering movements, and those of a thousand others like him, along the edges of crime wove the pattern of the underworld. Izzie didn't think of himself as a criminal. He was hurt by the fact that, at headquarters, there was a long list under the name of Izzie Norris, or Norton, or Martin, also known as Thin Izzie. He had never killed—and were he to, he would be instantly caught and killed in turn, for that was what happened to all those like Izzie.

Izzie's pale eyes moved more quickly under Deglin's steady gaze.

"You got some questions, chief?"

Deglin nodded. "I'm interested in the Scalise boys."

Izzie grinned. "Lotsa guys interested in the Scalise boys."

"They seem to have some quick money."

"They ain't telling where they picked it up, chief. Ain't breathing a word." He leaned forward. "What's up, chief?"

Deglin shook his head. "I just get very interested when guys like the Scalises show a lot of sudden dough. Running book?"

"You guys ought to know," Izzie said and laughed.

Deglin looked at him coldly.

"What do you mean?"

Izzie's eyes shifted and he stopped his laughter. "I was only kidding, chief," he said. "You know the talk? Bookies paying off? Only a joke."

"Don't joke," Deglin said evenly.

Izzie looked worried. Then he said. "Well, maybe I'm just as good off not having any money. When you got money your troubles begin."

"Are the Scalises having trouble?" Deglin said.

Izzie winked. "Mannie Scalise is. Gonna blow his dame."

"Which dame is that?"

"Oh, Christ, chief," Izzie said. "You know that blonde that used to be over in the Club Forty? Mannie wants to move up a notch and the word is he's blowing her."

"That'll be trouble?" Deglin asked.

Izzie grunted. "That blonde's a tough broad. She learns she's getting the finger instead of some of this nice new dough, and there's going to be some cutting."

Deglin nodded. "She still at the Forty?"

Izzie grinned with the sly pleasure that comes of talking about another guy's troubles.

"She will be when Mannie scratches her off the list. Right now he's got her stashed away in a hotel down in the Chelsea district."

Deglin didn't say anything for a minute, and Izzie's eyes moved quickly. The pleasure on his face faded.

"You a little short on dough these days?" Deglin said finally.

Izzie nodded. "You know how it is, chief." He sighed. "It's hard to come by and harder to keep."

Deglin pulled a bill from his pocket and tossed it across the table.

Izzie put it in his pocket without looking at it. "Thanks, chief. I'll get it back to you."

"No hurry," Deglin said.

It was the closing gambit. He waited for Izzie to say something and get up and leave. But Izzie's eyes only moved quickly from his glass to Deglin's face and back again.

"Had a case in the suburbs, eh, chief?"

"What?" Deglin said flatly.

Izzie looked at him, and his eyes turned away under the sudden hardness of Deglin's face. "Nothing," he said uncomfortably. "Guess I get to thinking all you guys do is work. Never figure you can have a little vacation yourself."

Deglin still looked at him steadily. "What do you mean?" he said.

Izzie's eyes moved more wildly. "Just that I was up in Harlem the other night. Late. Saw you coming out of the Hundred and Twenty-fifth Street station. Thought you'd been in the suburbs, carrying that big bag like you was."

The muscle in Deglin's jaw jumped and he rubbed it.

"What were you doing out there, Izzie?" he said, his voice casual.

Izzie grinned. "Little game. Nothing for you guys to get excited

NIGHT CRY

about. Just some friends. Penny ante."

"I'll bet," Deglin said.

Izzie decided suddenly he had talked too much. He got to his feet and nodded his head.

"Thanks for the loan, chief," he said.

Deglin nodded, still looking at him.

"See you?" Izzie asked.

Deglin nodded thoughtfully. "I'll see you," he said.

Izzie smiled, turned quickly, and went out of the saloon.

Deglin stared for a moment at the chair in which Izzie had sat. He looked up at the bartender and nodded to him, and the bartender brought over a drink. Deglin gave him a bill and the bartender took change from his pocket and counted it out laboriously. Then he went away and Deglin looked back at the chair and tasted his drink.

He'd been seen then. Izzie had seen him carrying the kitbag, so that in one mind in the city, Deglin was tied up with the kitbag. It could mean nothing or it could mean everything. Perhaps Izzie informed for someone else on the force. He didn't know, and there was no way he could find out. Izzie wouldn't say. The others on the force wouldn't say. But, in informing, Izzie had only to say another word—that he had seen Deglin carrying a big bag, a bag like Army officers had carried—and that might start it.

Deglin finished his drink. After he had left the saloon, one of the elderly men arguing at the end of the bar called the bartender over.

"Look, Mac," he said, looking at the drowsy white-haired man beside him, "that guy who just left. Wasn't that this detective, Deglin?"

The bartender moved the two beer glasses and mopped the bar and put the two beer glasses back.

"That was the guy," he said.

The elderly man leered triumphantly at his companion and the drowsy one opened his eyes and shrugged.

"I'm arguing?" he asked.

"Why, damn it all, you said—" the elderly man began—and the bartender returned to the middle of the bar and leaned back with his heavy elbows resting on the shelf. The way the detective had looked when he went out, the bartender decided, he was glad Devlin wasn't hunting for him. Then one of the customers signaled for another beer and the bartender drew it and mopped the bar before setting it down, the arguing of the two men at the end of the bar topping the murmuring of other voices.

11

The *Globe* handled the story in a manner much favored by the *Globe* editors, lightly and brightly, with just a gentle touch of the sarcasm they reserved for suburbanites whose penchant for play led them to small troubles.

Deglin read the piece on the way downtown the next morning. It did nothing to relieve the nagging worry over Izzie's knowledge that he had carried Paine's kitbag. If anything, the worry became deeper. There was little chance that Izzie would connect Paine's disappearance with the kitbag. He would have no reason to do it. Yet Deglin couldn't get the thin little man and his nervously shifting eyes out of his mind.

The story in the *Globe*, signed by Clement Smith, was a smart piece of research. It revealed a careful reference to the files of the newspaper, with special attention to the innuendoes of the society page. If what Smith reported was correct, and there was good reason to believe it was, Pete Redfield and Morgan Taylor had been more or less engaged several years before, a projected union which had been broken up first by Redfield's delight in playing around and more definitely by Morgan Taylor's enlistment as an Army nurse.

There was a reference to Morgan's comfortable and respectable parents and a conjecture as to what they felt about their daughter's selection of a gambling resort as a playground—if, indeed, some of their socially prominent friends had not themselves introduced the charming Morgan to the exclusive and richly appointed key club.

There was a reference to the blowoff Morgan and Paine had had in the club and to Paine's argument with Morrison, the dead "ancient playboy"—as Smith called him. Then, after a summing-up of the scrapes Paine had gotten into, a recountal of his whirlwind courtship of Morgan, the fact that the police had traced him to 125th Street Station, and the rather odd mystery of the well-heeled visitor who beat Pete Redfield to the apartment only to be touched for a loan.

And, finally, there was a picture—one taken some time before, Deglin imagined, and by a nightclub press agent. It showed Morgan, her hair dark against her bare shoulders, between Kendall Paine and Pete Redfield. There were glasses on the table in front of them, and while Morgan Taylor was smiling at the camera, both Pete Redfield and Ken Paine were looking at her.

The picture fitted the story perfectly. It was the final touch. Deglin folded the paper savagely. It meant that the other papers would handle it to a degree and that, instead of letting the search for Paine die of its own inertia, there would be pressure from the top.

When he arrived at 54th Street, he went directly to Knight's office, looking for some reaction to the *Globe* story. He found it at once. Knight was listening to two reporters from other newspapers and looking harried. Smith was over against the window, smiling faintly as a man from a rival tabloid talked in a hurt voice.

"It isn't that we mind Smith digging it up," he was saying, "but it would have been nice to tell us that you were holding up on the Morrison murder until you found Paine."

"Look," Knight said wearily. "I'm not holding up on anything. The DA is doing that. We know who killed Morrison and we got him dead to rights. And more than that, you know it."

"But why don't they do something about it?"

"That's the DA's job," Knight exploded.

"Or," said the *News* man with a cunning mildness, "is it an example of the inefficiency of the police department?"

Knight looked at him murderously. "I'd be careful, Joe," he said.

The *News* man smiled and nodded. Then he turned to Deglin. "Put Mark here on it," he said to Knight. "He can find Paine."

"For Christ's sake," Knight said. "Will you guys get out of here? He is on it."

The two newspapermen got up from their chairs and Clement Smith came away from the window. He looked at Deglin and his tired eyes were amused.

"What did you think of it, Mark?" he said.

"I didn't like it," Deglin said.

"But it is kind of a cute story."

NIGHT CRY

"It isn't worth a damn," Deglin said levelly, and watched the three men go out the door. Knight sat slackly in his chair, looking out through the window; then he shook his head and swung back around to his desk.

"With all the important things going on, those guys have to start a big stink about a guy taking a powder," he said.

"It'll die out," Deglin said.

Knight frowned. "There are some funny things about it," he said slowly. "That teletype from his sister in Massachusetts. She's worried about him. Plenty worried. And the fact that he's broke and then all of a sudden he's got a wad of dough."

"A wad?"

"He's buying big cab rides and railroad tickets. That's a wad for a guy who is flat an hour before. And why does he go clear to a Hundred and Twenty-fifth Street. He can get the same train at Grand Central."

Knight saw Deglin looking at him narrowly. He shook his head sharply and sighed. "Well," he said apologetically, "they've got me doing it, too." He pushed the papers around on his desk, his eyes intent, and then said, finally, "What about the waterfront stuff?"

"I haven't seen Klein yet. Don't know what he has."

"He phoned in," Knight said. "He's put together some stuff that makes it look like Scalise. One of the night watchmen they stuck up was seen with Scalise a month or so ago."

Deglin nodded. "I've got an angle on Scalise," he said.

"Good. What is it?"

Deglin told him about the blonde and Mamie Scalise.

"Sounds good," Knight agreed. "How do you do it?"

Deglin went to the window and stood there broodingly. "The precinct boys over in the warehouse district have been working on this?" he said.

Knight grunted and Deglin continued to look out the window. He had been thinking of Scalise and the blonde, but the picture had been washed out by one of Izzie's sneering face. Slowly there was forming the pattern of what he must do about that face. And what he had to do fitted neatly with what he should do about Scalise.

"I think I can help out the boys over there and wash it up for us too, Al," he said.

Knight watched him without comment.

"I'll have to do some checking first," Deglin said, finally turning from the window.

"Go to it," Knight said, and went back to the paper work that littered his desk.

Deglin made three phone calls and within a half hour his telephone rang and it was Izzie. His voice sounded muffled and far away as he asked for Deglin.

"It's Deglin," Deglin said.

"Oh, I called right away," Izzie said, his voice edged with curiosity. "Where are you?"

"In a phone booth."

"I can't tell you much, kid," Deglin said. "I just picked it up this morning. I'll try to run down some more dope today."

"What's that?" Izzie said.

Deglin was silent for a minute. "I think some of the boys have your number on the board."

"Oh, my God," Izzie said. The telephone hummed with his silence, and when he spoke again his voice was abject with fear. "Jesus, chief, what have I done."

"I don't know," Deglin said. "What have you done?"

"Nothing. Honest to God, chief. Not a damn thing."

"I heard maybe it's because you spring too many leaks," Deglin said.

Izzie cursed but his heart was not in it. His voice crooned with fear.

"What am I gonna do?" he said several times. "Who is it?"

"That's what I'm trying to find out. You'd better get yourself a rod, and you better lay low."

"I don't carry no rod. You know that, chief. I don't want get in no jam with the Sullivan law."

"You get yourself a gun," Deglin said.

"But what about the jam?"

"You got your jam," Deglin said sharply.

There was a long silence before Izzie said, "All right, chief. I'll get one."

"Good," Deglin said. "Where can I see you? Late."

"In my room," Izzie said. "I'm going in it and I ain't coming out."

NIGHT CRY

"No good," Deglin said quickly. "Look. I'll meet you on the dot of midnight." He gave him one of the deserted cross streets on the lower West Side. "At the corner of Eleventh," he said. "We can walk down the street and I can give you the dope."

"But—" Izzie began, and Deglin hung up.

He took some paper work down the corridor to an office in the uniformed men's division and shut himself in. Though he tried to set his mind on the reports, he found he couldn't. Instead, he smoked nervously and reviewed the schedule for the night. Around noon, he heard Riley's heavy voice outside the door and he remained silent. Riley called to someone, asking if he'd seen Mark Deglin, and when the indistinct answer came, Riley said, "If you see him, tell him I've run onto something. Want to talk to him about it."

Then his voice faded as he moved away and Deglin lit another cigarette. He didn't want Riley in on what was going to happen that night.

He had dinner at a small restaurant on the East Side. He wanted a couple of martinis first, but he didn't have them. Then, at about ten o'clock, he paid his check and got a cab outside, telling the driver to take him to the Flamingo Club. It was fashionable and expensive, and the discreet marquee said simply, "Presenting Jane Corby," as though that were enough to say about Jane Corby. And it was.

The headwaiter found Deglin a table over beside the piano, and smiled and commented that Mr. Deglin hadn't been in for several days.

"Busy, Conrad," Deglin explained. "I just want some coffee."

The headwaiter lifted his eyebrows and smiled. Then he raised his hand to a waiter and the waiter came hurrying over, nodded at the order and went to the kitchen fast. He had the coffee back, a silver pot of it, by the time the slim young piano player came to the center of the room and Jane Corby threaded her way between the tables, smiling to the right and the left until she looked at Deglin. Then she stopped smiling and went to the piano and looked at him once more, quietly, her eyes questioning.

She sang her songs, six of them, in her low throaty voice. They were ordinary songs but what she did to them was not ordinary. They became something special because of a special catch in her voice, a certain lilting sweetness that was there along with the throatiness.

When she had finished, she smiled at the room again and, as the applause swelled, nodded and said she'd be back and threaded her way out of the room again. Deglin finished his coffee, got up and followed her.

She was standing in her dressing room when he got there, waiting for him.

"Hello, Jane," he said soberly.

"Hello, Mark."

He closed the door behind him and leaned against it, looking at her. She didn't smile, nor was there anything in her eyes at all.

"I waited for a couple of days," he began. "I think you know I'm sorry."

"It's all right, Mark," she said without inflection.

"Thanks," he said. He came away from the door.

"Your show was better tonight," he said. "I liked that new song. The one you close with. I hadn't heard it."

"A publisher brought it around last week," she said. "It's nice."

He smiled then. "It's nice when you sing it, Janie," he said.

She was still erect and noncommittal, but the completeness of her rejection had been dissipated, as though she were finding a resolution she had determined to keep fading swiftly to smoke. She went to the dressing table and did some quick unimportant things to her make-up.

"I should get back," she said.

"Not for fifteen minutes, Janie," he said.

She stopped the unimportant things. "That's right, Mark."

"I had to see you, Jane. I need you."

She turned against the dressing table, slowly.

"Do you want to see me anymore, Jane?" he said urgently.

The protest was quick in her soft eyes. "Yes, Mark," she said.

He came across to her. "Then I can tell you," he said. "I was with you two nights ago—from one o'clock on. It's important."

"Is something wrong, Mark?" she asked.

The muscle in his jaw worked. "There may be, Janie," he said.

"You were with me," she said.

He nodded and touched her arm. "You're my girl, Jane," he said.

NIGHT CRY

She looked up at him then. "When will I see you, Mark?" she asked softly. Her lips parted slightly.

"I'll be home around one," he said.

She smiled at him then and touched his cheek. "I have to get back on," she said—and her voice was a caress.

Deglin left the Flamingo. Again he took a cab, though this time to an address deep in the West Side. The side street, dark and deserted, was lighted only by two street lamps and by the faint blue lights of a precinct station. A wet, cold wind had come up off the river, and it carried the lonesome sounds of the river traffic in to compete with the low always present turbulence of the city.

At the desk, Deglin asked if Postliagni was around, and the desk sergeant looked up from a paper and waved his thumb at a door. Deglin went through it and found the big saturnine detective with his feet on a desk, talking on a telephone. He nodded at Deglin and, still listening, winked. "Okay," he said finally, and put the phone back in its cradle.

"Hiya, Mark," he said.

"Hello, Mike," Deglin said.

"What brings you into the wilderness?"

"You're on that waterfront stuff, aren't you?" Deglin said.

Postliagni scowled. "And brother, what a bitched-up thing *that* is," he said.

"Knight asked Klein and me to look around," Deglin said. "We dug some stuff."

Postliagni nodded and rubbed his big nose. "I heard you were doing something," he said. "Christ, we know who's doing it, but we can't nail them."

"Would you like to?" Deglin asked.

"Give me a chance," Postliagni said simply.

"Well," Deglin said, "there may be something in this. There may not. But you have a better excuse than I to look into it."

Postliagni rubbed his nose again.

"I understand Mannie Scalise is shedding that blonde of his," Deglin said. "Only she don't know it."

The big detective sat up. "That straight?" he said.

"Straight as I can get it," Deglin said. "I was thinking that if you were just to bump into this blonde and needle her a little bit on it, she might—" He left it unfinished, and Postliagni grinned and nodded.

"She's a rough dame," he agreed.

"That's what I'd heard," Deglin said.

"You don't want to do this?" Postliagni was puzzled. "It might break it, kid."

"You do it, Mike," Deglin said.

Postliagni nodded. "First time I ever heard you didn't want to talk to a blonde," he said, grinning.

They talked until ten minutes of twelve, and then Deglin got to his feet, touched the brim of his hat at Postliagni, and started out.

"Want one of the boys to run you over?" Postliagni asked. Deglin shook his head. "I'll walk," he said.

He went outside, back into the sounds and the feel of the river. He stopped on the sidewalk, the wind driving steadily against his face, and he said to himself carefully.

Have you got it now?

You have only to be sure Izzie has the gun, and you're in. You have only to be sure it appears that Izzie was doing something he shouldn't have been doing, and that you caught him at it. The fact that you shot him? It'll be self-protection—the simplest, most obvious kind of self-protection. It'll even be heroic. A sample of Deglin's vigilance and his courage, shooting it out with a known criminal who was in the act of burglarizing.

And it won't matter that Izzie will appear to be making armed entry on whatever loft building you choose as the most convenient....

Nor will it matter that, as Izzie dies, he will be frightened and puzzled and sick....

Then Deglin stopped thinking actively.

He went across to Eleventh Avenue and turned down it, his hands deep in his topcoat pockets, his collar up against the wind. The noises of the city were an undercurrent, the varying sounds of the river desolate and ominous. Blocks down, Izzie's figure detached itself from the shadows of a doorway and moved quickly beside him.

"Hello," Deglin said softly. "You've got the gun?"

"I got one," Izzie said—and his voice was a hoarse whisper.

Deglin turned off on one of the side streets and Izzie turned with

NIGHT CRY 109

him, bumping him in his haste to keep alongside, not to be more than a step from Deglin.

"Chief, did you find anything?"

"Yes," Deglin said. "They want you. The Costellos."

"The Costellos?" Izzie's words were a sob of protest. "Christ, I ain't never done anything against the Costellos."

"I don't know anything about that."

Izzie walked silently, his head shaking slowly. He put a hand to his face and sobbed shudderingly.

"I gotta get out of town," he said. "I gotta."

Far back on the darkened street, ringing faintly from the blank, unlighted windows of the huge loft buildings, came the sound of footsteps. Deglin touched Izzie's arm and pulled him quickly to the shadows of an areaway.

"Were you followed?" he asked, and Izzie's arm trembled under his hand.

"I dunno," he mumbled.

"Get down the stairs," Deglin said softly.

Izzie stumbled down and Deglin followed, straining his eyes in the darkness. He was shaking slightly, trembling with excitement. He could feel his breath coming quickly through his mouth. "Get your gun out," he said into the blackness ahead—and as the faint fumbling sounds came to him, he took his own revolver from its shoulder holster. The measured footsteps rang louder in the street. Deglin, his body faced toward Izzie, did not look back. The footsteps rang clear at the entrance to the areaway and began to diminish. The long areaway was beginning to assume shape in Deglin's eyes—a greyness that became darker where Izzie shrank against the wall. The distant footsteps faded out and the darkness moved.

"Izzie," Deglin said, his voice bright and hard.

Izzie's voice trembled with relief. "Yeah, chief?"

"You've got your chance, Izzie," Deglin said. "Shoot."

The darkness was frozen. "Good God," the sobbing words came.

"You've got your chance," Deglin said again. Excitement welled in him so that he shook violently. "Shoot, you son-of-a-bitch." He could see Izzie's eyes, whitely.

Then slowly the blackness slid down and Izzie's racking sobs came out of the greyness. He swore, the curses meaningless and sick-sounding.

For a moment, Deglin held the gun on him, then it dropped to his side. He went to Izzie and kicked him.

"You miserable yellow bastard," he said, his voice shaking.

Izzie stirred.

"I want you out of town," Deglin said. "I would have killed you now, but you're a yellow cur. If I see you again, I will kill you. And I'll look for you. All the time."

Izzie's racking sobs came to him as he turned away. He went up the stairs and down the street, almost sobbing himself with anger and frustration.

An hour later, when he got to his apartment, Jane Corby was already there. She got to her feet as he opened the door, and she came to him quickly. He waited slackly, his head lowered.

"Mark," she said.

He let her get him out of his topcoat and went without speaking to the sofa before the fireplace. She brought him a drink and he shook his head and sat, his eyes dark and brooding. Finally, when he shook his head hard and then ran his hands into his hair and sat that way, crouched in the chair, she took her coat and, still looking at him, went out the door.

12

The bedside phone brought Deglin out of a nightmarish sleep the next morning. He took it from its cradle at once and held it while he looked blankly at the greying windows of the bedroom, and then at his watch. It was seven o'clock. He lay back and put the phone to his ear.

"Yes?" he said into the receiver.

"Mark?" the worn voice asked.

"Yeah. Who is it?"

"Knight," the voice said. It was tired and upset. "Can you get down here pretty quick?"

"What's doing?" Deglin asked. He was fully awake now and he looked at the ceiling, waiting for the answer.

"I tried to get you last night," Knight said. "But you were out."

"On the Scalise thing," Deglin explained. "It may work."

"It has worked. We just got a call. Mike Postliagni followed it right up and the dame spilled the works. But this isn't that."

"What is it?" Deglin said.

"Something Riley dug up," Knight said. "I'm having the Taylor girl brought in."

"Oh," Deglin said. He kept his eyes on the ceiling and he had the feeling of sickness again. "I'll be right down."

Knight hung up.

Deglin got out of bed and went into the bathroom and showered. After he had toweled himself off, he lathered his face and started to shave, but he found his hand was shaking. He tried twice to get the razor started down his lean dark cheek but finally he had to use the styptic pencil and wash the lather from his face. He dressed and, after stopping at the corner drugstore for a cup of coffee, grabbed a cab.

Clement Smith was in the anteroom outside Knight's office, looking quarrelsome and suspicious. He stopped Deglin on the way across to Knight's door.

"What are they doing with Morgan Taylor in there?" he demanded.

"She came down?"

"She's in there with Riley and Knight," Smith said.

Deglin looked at him, his own mind seething with questions. "Maybe it's your goddamn story," he said tightly.

Smith scowled. Then he turned and went back to a chair and sat in it, pulling a folded newspaper from his topcoat pocket.

"I think," Deglin said, "you'd better get back to your own damned office. There's a place for you guys and it isn't here."

Smith looked at him wordlessly. Then he folded the newspaper again, put it back in his pocket, and slouched out. Deglin watched him go, then went to Knight's office and pushed open the door. Knight was behind the desk, looking absently at some papers in front of him. Riley was at the window, half-seated on the ledge. Morgan Taylor sat in a chair opposite Knight. When Deglin walked in, she looked at him, smiling warmly.

"Good morning, Miss Taylor," he said. He nodded at Riley and Knight.

Knight got out of his chair at once.

"You'll excuse me, Miss Taylor," he said, and when she nodded, he went by Deglin and stood in the outer office until Deglin came out too. He closed the door.

"What in the hell is going on?" Deglin said.

"I wanted to fill you in before we talk to her. I don't know what it is, and it's possible that she won't tell us much."

Deglin waited.

"Riley did some checking around yesterday. He can tell you about it later. He found a witness who saw someone carrying something out of Paine's."

"Paine carried the bag out," Deglin said softly.

"This witness saw Paine, too. What this character carried was big. And heavy."

Deglin said nothing for a moment. His mind raced in a search for witnesses. He hadn't been seen. He could swear to it. He'd been careful. Only Kendall Paine had been seen.

"What's she got to do with it?" he asked finally.

"I don't know." Knight shook his head. "But she was there much later. Much after Paine was supposed to have left."

NIGHT CRY

"*Supposed* to have left?" Deglin said sharply.

"Witnesses saw him in the cab and at the Hundred and Twenty-fifth Street station."

"Maybe it wasn't him. The girl was seen going back into his place late—maybe three, maybe four. We don't know. Look, do you want to talk to Riley?"

Deglin studied it. Should he talk to Riley now, or should he wait and see what Riley had? Would it be better to talk after he had learned more about what Riley had—and how he had found it?

"Why don't we talk to her now?"

Knight nodded and led the way back into the office. She had been talking to Riley, and Riley had been listening with polite interest. They looked up together and she smiled as Knight went around his desk to his chair.

"I might tell you now, Mr. Knight," she said, "that if you are in touch with Ken, you can tell him that the first move is his. Like checkers."

"We haven't been in touch with Mr. Paine," Knight said.

She stopped smiling.

"We appreciate it when people come in, as you have, in order to give us information," Knight went on.

She didn't say anything. She was puzzled and a little taken aback at his quiet, heavy voice.

"After you left Mr. Paine," Knight said, "did you go directly home?"

"No," she answered slowly.

"What did you do?"

"I walked."

"At what time did you get home?"

She looked at him uncertainly for an instant and then finally she smiled. When his face stayed impassive, her smile lessened and she turned to Riley. Riley was looking at his fingernails absently. Her smile fled.

"I don't know," she said.

"Did you go back to Paine's room?" Knight asked.

She was going to answer it. She was going to tell him something but she decided against it. She said, "May I ask what his is about, Mr. Knight?"

He studied her for a moment. "Maybe I've been a little blunt,

114   WILLIAM L. STUART

Miss Taylor," he said, pleasantly. "You know we have been looking for Mr. Paine. Our reason for wanting to find him is that we feel that he may have seen something that will, beyond question, substantiate the confession we have from Carlstrom."

"He didn't," she said.

Knight nodded. "However," he said carefully, "it is still a possibility we must cover. He has not yet told us so. He had a fight with a man who was murdered a few minutes later. He left, and has now disappeared. Anyway, we haven't found him. You say he had nothing to do with it. You're right, because we know who did it and how he did it. And yet we have a job to do here. Lieutenant Deglin is charged with the proper handling of the case because it falls in this district. Detective Riley is assigned to it from Homicide. They must follow every piece of evidence, every possible new piece, until the case is brought to trial." His heavy voice stopped and he looked at her gravely. "Therefore," he said soberly, "when we find that things may not have gone as we had understood they had gone, we have to look into them."

She had recaptured her poise. She smiled at him pleasantly. "However," she said, "I haven't done anything."

"We know of nothing," Knight said politely.

She smiled at Deglin and at Riley, too.

"Then," she said, "because I regard it as a rather personal matter, I would prefer not to say what happened after Ken and I left the gambling place."

She looked from him to Riley and then at Deglin.

"Thanks for coming in," Knight said.

She got to her feet, smiling. But she didn't speak again. She went to the door and closed it quietly behind her. Deglin said nothing, his eyes moving from Riley to Knight. Knight regarded Riley for a minute and then said, grumblingly, "Well, she's right."

Riley nodded.

"What the hell is this?" Deglin asked impatiently.

Knight sighed. "Tell him, Dan," he said.

Riley looked at his fingernails again, then pushed his hat forward and scratched the back of his head. "I looked for you yesterday, Mark," he began. "Thought we could check into it a little more. When I couldn't find you, I told Knight."

NIGHT CRY

"Yes," Deglin said.

"I was down around Paine's apartment yesterday, just checking around. I decided I might as well ask a question or two of the neighbors."

Deglin waited.

"Well, there wasn't much, except this old lady. She lives on the second floor of the building across the street."

"She'd seen something?" Deglin asked, his words furry in his ears. He remembered with shocking clarity the moving curtain in the second-story window.

"She seen plenty, that old dame." Riley wagged his head. "That's all she *does* is see things."

Deglin heard it then in Riley's slow words. She had seen someone go into Paine's apartment, sometime after Paine himself had come home with the girl. This person was a stranger whom she did not recognize. Then, a short time later, she saw Paine come out—though she did not think it was Paine.

"She didn't think it was Paine?" Deglin said sharply.

Riley had a notebook out and he examined a page. "Yeah," he said, raising his head and nodding. "She said it looked like Paine all right and he had a bandage on his eye like the paper said, but he didn't wave to her."

"Didn't *wave* to her?" Deglin said.

"Yeah," Riley said. "Whenever Paine sees her sitting in the window, he waves to her. Never misses, like a ritual. This guy looks at her, she says, but he doesn't wave."

Deglin looked at Knight, who lifted his shoulders and dropped them, and said, "There's more yet."

"Well," Riley said, referring again to the notebook, "later in the night—she don't know what time—she sees this dame, Morgan Taylor, going back into the house. She hasn't seen her come out."

"Come out?" Deglin asked.

"Yeah. She'd gone in with Paine when he first gets home, but the old lady don't see her come out, she only sees her go back in much later. She explains that she likes to get up and have tea so she can't see *everything*. Then, later, she sees someone come out of Paine's again. Only this time it's so foggy she can't really tell much about them except that it takes the party a long time to get out of the building and the party is carrying something heavy. *Big* and heavy." He closed the notebook and slid it into a hip pocket.

Knight got out of his chair, as though he'd made up his mind about something. "I ain't been from behind that desk for a week," he said.

Deglin watched him, not moving in his chair. Riley watched him also. Knight nodded ponderously. "Might as well get some air," he explained. "Paine's apartment has to be looked at again—after this."

13

In the car on the way to Paine's apartment, Knight, sitting heavily between Riley and Deglin, congratulated Deglin on the Scalise case.

"It was awful neat, Mark," he said admiringly. "Awful neat."

Deglin nodded and said nothing.

The driver pulled the car up at the curb of the house on the side street, deserted in its one-block length in spite of the grinding traffic of the waterfront only yards away. Another car arrived at the curb almost directly after they did, and from it emerged four additional plainclothesmen, the lab men of the department, whom Knight had called in from headquarters. A prowl car, called on the radio, was already there and the two uniformed men stood at the entrance of the building with the janitor, who was frightened and quiet.

One of the patrolmen came down to the sedan and, putting one elbow against the opened window, stuck his head partly into the car.

"Nobody's been in the room since our guys looked at it," he said to Knight. "Paine's rent's paid, but he didn't hire any maid service, the spic says." The patrolman grinned.

Knight grunted. "Wonder one of you hasn't tried to rent it."

"Not down here, Inspector," the patrolman said and, still grinning, backed away from the car while Deglin opened the door and they got out.

They went up to the room and, as Deglin walked in, the flood of memory was overpowering. It was as he had left it: the mussed bed, the littered desk, the bottle of whisky and the glass still half full. The carmine-lipstick cigarette butt was still in the dirty ashtray. Deglin looked around slowly, the muscle in his jaw twitching. Were this another room, another case, his mind would have been clear, driving and inquiring in the way in which it had been trained. But in this room, it was as though his mind were encased in a sealed box, blank and seamless. His thoughts scurried aimlessly, starting on a line, then stopping almost as soon as they had begun, defeated.

Knight was at the drawers of the bureau, pulling them open, taking out the few articles of clothing they held, looking at them thoughtfully. The others—Riley and the lab men—stood as Deglin himself stood, watching.

Knight finished with the drawers and then went to the littered desk. He pawed through the papers, looking at several, puzzling over one at length.

"What's this?" he said finally to Deglin, and Deglin moved over beside him and took the sheet of paper. It was half-covered with writing.

"Looks like a part of a book," he said.

"Oh," Knight said, and dismissed it.

He moved idly around the room for a minute and then the ashtray caught his eye. He picked up the reddened cigarette end and regarded it for a moment.

"The old lady across the street says she didn't see the Taylor girl come out?" he said.

Riley moved over to his side and looked at the cigarette, too.

"Yeah," he said. "But then, she wasn't watching all the time."

Knight nodded. "Any other way out of here?" he asked, and walked over and opened the closet door. He poked around in it for a minute and came out again. Then he went to the single window in the back recess, a window that overlooked a small court and a single tree that waved its remaining smudged and tattered leaves frantically in the wind.

"Doesn't look like any way out here," he said, and raised the window. He held it for a minute, looking out into the rectangle of dirt and grey crabgrass, and the sounds of the wind and the traffic along the riverfront flooded into the room. Then he took his hands from the window and it fell with a crash that was an exclamation point cutting off the sounds from outside.

The others jumped. But not Deglin. He had expected it, agonizingly. And now he stood by the bed, his body slack, while Riley went to the window and pulled at one of the sash cords. It came easily from the pulley at the top of the sash, and Riley examined the cut end of it. Then Knight was pulling out the other

NIGHT CRY

sash cord and looking at it, and Deglin was forcing himself to move across the room toward them.

"Cut within the last couple days," Knight said, almost to himself.

"Yeah," Riley said. He let go the window cord and turned to the men who had moved over behind them. One picked up the cord and looked at it, pursing his lips. "Jack," Riley said to him, "go get that superintendent."

They waited without talking until the superintendent came into the room, his small dark face more composed and his eyes more distressed.

"This window usually have sashweights?" Riley said to him at once.

"*Si*. Yes," the little man said courteously.

"You ain't taken them out of this window here?" Riley asked.

"No. Why?" The little man shrugged.

"Okay." Riley said.

The little man looked at him, and then Riley said, "Okay, you can beat it," and the little man looked relieved and turned and left.

Knight rubbed his hand across his mouth. "Two of them," he said. "They sure wanted to make sure something stayed sunk, Dan."

Riley didn't answer. He regarded the rope end again speculatively. "That there Taylor girl is a nice girl," he said regretfully.

Deglin was startled. "The Taylor girl?" he said involuntarily.

Knight looked at him bleakly. He put his head close to the window sash, looking at it, then he said quietly, "Right here on this side." Deglin looked, trying not to find too quickly the marks where the wooden board had been pried away.

"They're here on this side," Riley said, pointing.

Knight nodded. He turned to the men who watched. "You guys can go to work. I want any prints you can find—and then follow them up. There may be something in Washington."

One of the men began opening a bag he carried, and Knight said to Riley and Deglin, "Let's take a walk."

They said nothing as they went down the stairs and out of the building. Knight shook his head at the uniformed chauffeur when he began to open the car door for them, and they walked on past the car and around the corner to the street under the elevated highway along the riverfront.

Traffic streamed unendingly in front of them, rumbling and grinding in the shadows of the giant pillars. They waited for a break and moved across. They passed the ferry entrance and at the tugboat slip they stopped. They stood there on the wooden piling, still without speaking.

"Whatever it is," Knight said finally, "it's probably in here."

Deglin looked at the water. It moved uncomfortably, green and oily, as though conscious of its secret.

"I didn't see any other place where you could get to the river. Not easy," Knight said after a minute.

Deglin kept his head lowered. She's a nice girl, that Taylor girl, he thought, and what did Riley mean? It came to him slowly, as he looked at the surging water at his feet. It was not he who had placed that burden there. He was the passerby. The figure without substance that was there and then faded. To have a murder there must be motive. There must be background and thought, the burning of passions and of hate, of throat-aching disappointment, of deep red ambition. The passerby could not have those. He was ephemeral, of no body. To the coldly seeking Knight, the factual plodding Riley, he could not exist.

"Yes," Deglin said. "This looks like the only place."

Knight looked once more at the moving backwash of the river. Then his gaze went up and across, past a hustling tug, a laboring barge, a distant ferry sweeping slowly across the green-grey river, and finally to the brown heights of New Jersey, bleak in the cold light. He turned then, and Deglin and Riley followed him through a break in the traffic and up to the short side street. At the car they stopped.

Deglin said, "You'll get the harbor patrol, Al? I guess Dan and I had better talk to people around here again."

Knight nodded. "We ought to have something more before we put a big team on it," he agreed.

Deglin rubbed his chin. "Good enough," he said. He looked at Riley. "We got Dan to thank for this."

Riley shook his head. His big face was sober and his eyes were withdrawn and intent. "Maybe I ain't so glad, Mark," he said. "I like that Taylor girl."

They started back toward the building then, leaving Knight, but

NIGHT CRY

when they were almost at the stairs, Knight spoke.

"Hey, Mark."

Deglin turned. Knight was already in the car and was leaning forward so that his head was at the opened window. Deglin walked back to him.

"I'm glad to see you got it straightened out," Knight said.

Deglin looked at him, conscious of the muscle in his jaw, not touching it.

Knight's eyes were searching. "You had a scrap with your girl," he said.

Deglin nodded slowly.

Knight nodded, too, heavily and with satisfaction.

"You ain't been yourself, Mark," he said. "I'm glad you got it straightened out."

Then he leaned back in his seat and the car moved away from the curb.

14

Riley was up in the room. He was watching one of the laboratory men repack his little bag. His face was still quiet.

"What did they get?" Deglin asked.

Riley lifted his eyes. "Quite a bit," he said softly. "There were prints on the window sash."

Deglin said nothing.

"And on some glasses and the bathroom fixtures," Riley went on. "The guy here says they're pretty good."

"Then he can follow through on them," Deglin said, remembering the gloves he himself had worn, the precautions he had taken.

"We'll start with the old lady across the street?" Deglin said after a minute.

"She knows the most," Riley said. "Maybe we can make a timetable out of it."

"Yes," Deglin agreed.

They went down the stairs and across the narrow street and Riley led the way up the dark, musty-smelling stairs of the rickety three-story building. He rapped several times in the darkness and a thin voice sounded muffled. The darkness lightened suddenly as Riley pushed a door open.

The room was quiet and musty. It smelled faintly of mice and of ancient tea. The furniture was cracked and its upholstery grey with age and wear. There was no bed in the room, so there must be another room, dark and tiny, behind it. The woman was in a chair at one of the two front windows, and the position of the chairs and of a narrow, stained pad that cushioned the sill, indicated that she spent a great share of her time there. She was small and quick in her movements and though her face was mottled and wrinkled, her eyes were bright as a terrier's.

"This is Mr. Deglin of the force," Riley said heavily. "Mrs. Meacham, Mark."

Deglin took off his hat. Riley saw him do it, started to take his off,

NIGHT CRY **123**

but left it on anyway. The old woman smiled sharply, showing long, startlingly white teeth so even they seemed drawn in her mouth. She turned her head slightly and regarded Deglin.

"I've seen you," she said in her tiny voice.

"You have?" Deglin said. His voice was careful. "I was here the other evening. Over there." He looked across the street. "Some minutes after Paine left."

"I don't mean there," the old woman said. "In the papers. Your picture's been in the papers lots."

Deglin smiled at her. "Mr. Riley tells me you saw quite a bit the other night."

The perfect teeth showed again, briefly. "Old people don't sleep much, young man. I often wish the room faced the other way so I could watch the river. Like them little boats and everything. But I guess this has to be. Couldn't see the river anyway with all them wharfs and the highway." She looked at him, her ancient head still cocked like a puppy's, her eyes bright.

"We'd like to go over what you saw again with you," Deglin said. "Get it straight in our minds."

She bobbed her head.

"About what time did you see Paine and the girl, Morgan Taylor, the first time?"

She smiled. "Young man, you won't find any clocks in here, excepting your own. I can tell when it's day by looking out the window and when I'm hungry by how I feel. When you get old like me, you don't care much about what time it is."

Deglin frowned briefly. "But you did see them go into the house across the way?"

"Sure. I've seen her a lot. I know him, too. He always waves at me."

"And that's why you didn't think the man with the bandage actually was young Paine?"

"Well, he didn't wave at me. He looked up here, all right, but he didn't wave."

She was enjoying it. She knew what she saw and what she didn't see, and there was an air about her that she was going to tell exactly that. She would make a believable witness.

"Did you see anyone between the times you saw Paine go in with the girl and Paine come out?"

"Yes," she said. "Another man. But I didn't see him come out."

"Could he have been going to another of the rooms in the building?"

"I don't know," she said. "He don't live there, though. I'd recognize him if he lived there."

"How would you describe this other one?" Riley said slowly.

She turned to him and her wrinkled lips pursed. "The fog was beginning a little," she said.

"Big? Little? Fat? Skinny?"

"Big, I suppose," she said.

Riley put it in his notebook and then waited for Deglin to start again.

"You didn't see anyone again for some time?" Deglin said.

"I made myself some tea and had some toast."

"So it was some time before you came back to the window here?"

"Quite a long time," she agreed. "I like to sit over my tea."

"And then you saw—"

"The girl again, going in."

"You hadn't seen her come out?"

"I saw her go in—and then I saw her go in again. So she must've come out."

"That's right," Deglin said smiling.

"Did you see her come out again?"

"Not rightly so," the old lady said. "I dozed off a little."

"But you did see something more?"

"I woke up and it was foggy. Real foggy, young man. And I saw someone coming out. Took them a long time. And they carried something big."

"Was it the girl?"

"I don't know," she said. "I couldn't tell who it was."

Deglin looked at Riley and then back at her. She looked as if she had more to say, and he asked her, "Is there anything more?"

"What's it about, young feller?" she asked. "I saw in the papers the boy has run away."

"We don't know yet," Deglin said. "It may be, though, that we'll ask you to come down to the station and tell that again, and maybe look at some people. Will that be all right, Mrs. Meacham?"

The frown deepened the wrinkles of her face. "How would I get

NIGHT CRY   **125**

over there?" she asked.

"We'd drive you over and drive you back."

"Not in one of them black-and-white prowl cars!" She said it warningly.

"In a limousine."

She nodded. Her face tightened in a hundred-thousand wrinkles and her laugh cackled. "Neighbors would think I had me a house here if they saw me getting into one of them black-and-white things." She cackled thinly some more and then took a tiny handkerchief from a pocket of her apron and wiped her bright eyes.

Deglin and Riley got to their feet. They smiled and Deglin put his hat on. She waved a bony hand at them and looked out the window. As they closed the door, her laughter had started again. They went down the dark stairs.

At the street, Riley said, "Knight's probably got the harbor patrol at work by now."

"It's been twenty minutes or so," Deglin agreed.

They moved along the street to its end and across the heavy traffic of the waterfront. They could see the dark superstructure of the police tug even as they passed the ferry building.

A mob of people streamed suddenly out of the ferry as they came abreast of it and Riley and Deglin waited for the hurrying throng to pass. The people looked neither to the right nor to the left, moving fast, ignoring the boat in the slip and the silently working men on its deck. Deglin felt that he was again breathing through his mouth, and there was perspiration on his forehead and under his arms and on his back in spite of the sharp wind off the river. He closed his mouth and, when the crowd of hurrying ferry passengers thinned, followed Riley to the tug slip.

They stood for a few minutes on the wooden stringpiece.

"We could stand here all day," Deglin said urgently.

"I guess so," Riley agreed.

"We should get back," Deglin said.

Riley turned willingly enough but there was a sudden exclamation from someone on the boat, and the activity of the men moving on its deck increased. After a moment, the body came out of the water, slowly, oily with viscous mud, the dirty water cascading back from its blanket shroud. Deglin felt his stomach revolt, and he caught the vomit in his mouth, held it and swallowed convulsively.

"Damn it to hell," Riley said with sad bitterness. "Oh, damn it to hell."

The body moved up, smearing the side of the boat with its filth, the sashweights dripping mud as they came out of the water. Deglin swallowed convulsively again.

Then Riley turned from the water and started back. "We might as well go in, Mark," he said. "The others in the building can wait now."

Deglin turned and followed him. They waited for a cab until one discharged a passenger at the ferry and then they went back to 54th Street. Knight was in his office, rapping the ends of his blunt fingers on the desk, his face grey and displeased, his eyes clouded.

"Well," he said, looking at them, "I just got the call through from the Telegraph Bureau. Paine has come back, all right."

"We were there," Riley said.

"He wasn't shot or knifed. He was hit. Hard."

Riley and Deglin took chairs. They said nothing. Knight's fingers continued to drum on the desk. They made a strong, thudding sound. "I've already talked to the DA."

They still said nothing.

"He wants this one right away. That story Smith wrote's got everybody watching it. The mayor right on down. This one we gotta get quick."

They were silent.

"And we're going to get it," Knight said, his fingers thudding, his voice storming. "We're looking like fools. A guy is knocked off and we're taken in by the oldest dodge in the world. If it hadn't been for Riley, dammit, we'd never of gotten onto it."

Riley did nothing. He had been looking out the window. He continued to look out the window.

"I gotta call out for this Redfield guy," Knight said. "I don't know how long before we can get this girl in. She's out in Connecticut, I guess. We'll get her. Tell me about the old lady. Did you go there?"

He looked at Deglin. Deglin nodded.

"Riley's got the notes," he said. "We couldn't get any timetable. She doesn't believe in clocks."

NIGHT CRY

"You were there after the guy who must've been dressed in Paine's clothes left. That'll give us a start. What time did you call me?"

"I didn't notice," Deglin said.

"Good Christ," Knight exploded. "Don't you believe in clocks, either?"

Deglin didn't say anything and Knight looked disgusted and turned to Riley. He started to ask him what things looked like but the door opened and there was Pete Redfield, big and scowling and worried, with a plainclothes man.

"This is Redfield, chief," the detective said.

Knight changed instantly. The stormy look left his eyes, his fingers stilled on the desk, his body straightened slightly. He didn't smile, but his face suddenly had a look as though things were all right and this was little more than a visit.

"Hello, Mr. Redfield," he said.

Redfield's face lost its scowl. He still looked curious and alert when he sat down opposite Knight but he was ready to talk.

"Reason we asked you to come in," Knight said, "was that we'd like to check your actions of two nights ago."

'They were in the papers," Redfield said.

Knight nodded, his manner still calm.

"We'd like to get a little more."

"Go ahead," Redfield said. "What do you want to know?"

"You went in to Paine's room and he wasn't there. Does he normally leave his door unlocked?"

"I suppose not," Redfield said.

"But you weren't surprised to find it unlocked?"

"He'd called me and asked me to come over. I thought he expected me."

"No one let you into the room, then?"

Redfield was surprised. "There was no one there. Ken had gone. I told you that."

"You were a good friend of Paine's, to be running over on a bad night to lend him money."

"Sure I—" He stopped and looked at Knight. "I still am," he said sharply. "Ken's a good guy. Been a little hard to handle these last couple of months but he's a good guy."

"That's why you've had to smack him a couple of times."

"Once," said Redfield.

Knight looked at him carefully. "What did you do after you left Paine's?"

Redfield wasn't going to answer. He was getting sore and was going to blow his top. Riley saw it. He prodded him gently.

"Okay, Redfield," he said. "We haven't got all day."

"For Christ's sake—" Redfield began.

Knight cut in sharply. "Paine's dead, bud. We found him in the river."

There was a long silence. Redfield looked steadily at him.

His anger had gone, and he looked rock-like and cold. "The poor devil," he said.

"So where did you go after you left his place?" Knight said.

"I went home. To my room uptown. Read."

"You didn't by any chance go to the Hundred and Twenty-fifth Street station?"

Redfield knew suddenly what he meant. His lips whitened and he looked quickly at Deglin and at Riley. "No, I didn't," he said. "I went home."

"Anybody see you go into your room?"

Redfield looked at him. He wasn't frightened yet but he moistened his lips. "I don't think so," he said quietly.

"We're going to have to hold you," Knight said. "Until we can get some things straightened around."

Redfield rubbed his hand across his eyes with an abrupt, quick motion. "I can get a lawyer," he said.

"Sure," Knight said.

"Believe me, I had nothing to do with this—whatever you're talking about."

"We'll see," Knight said without emotion. He turned to Riley. "Take care of him, Dan. Make the charge. And you'd better let him get to the law right away."

Riley got out of his chair and stood beside Redfield, looking down at him. Redfield looked up at him. He tried to smile and managed a fairly good one. Then he got up and looked again at Knight and at Deglin. He followed Riley out, walking only a pace behind him.

Deglin sat silently, not turning his head to the door, not watching Knight. The small room was quiet for a long space. There were the

NIGHT CRY   **129**

distant ringing of telephones muffled by the door and the spaced clack of a typewriter somewhere. A voice sounded heavy and indistinct. The department was moving evenly and methodically, looking at another murder in a thousand murders or another larceny in ten thousand or another of any of the millions of things it worked with all year long—as factually as a factory looks at its steel bumpers or rubber pants or cans of corn.

"We're going to have to have luck with the girl," Knight said. "The papers have got it already."

Deglin had trouble getting the words out. "Have they tried her home?"

"She isn't there. She's nowhere," Knight said.

Deglin looked at him finally. Knight's fingers were again moving on the desk, lightly, so that they made no sound. The phone rang and his fingers stopped their motions. He picked up the receiver and grunted his name. Then he listened, grunting occasionally, and put the receiver back.

"DA's office," he said. "They want a meeting on this tomorrow morning."

Deglin found himself running his hand across his jaw again and again. He stopped with an effort. "Have you put out a call? On the girl?" He said it slowly, carefully.

"No," said Knight. "Take care of it, will you?"

"We can get that picture the *Globe* ran," Deglin said. We'll stat it and get enough to show the cruisers and the precincts."

"And the DA's office wants the complete report. This afternoon," Knight said.

Deglin nodded and got to his feet. "Riley and I'll write it up right away," he said.

He went out of the office, glad to go, leaving Knight again drumming his fingers on his desk, his eyes unhappy, his mouth set and grim.

Deglin found Riley and they went around the corner for coffee. They said nothing to each other. Riley was morose, lost in his own thoughts. He stirred his coffee slowly, regarding the row of pies on the back counter. Then he shook his head and sighed and looked into the coffee cup.

"The DA's office wants a report on the whole thing," Deglin told him finally.

Riley nodded.

"We'd better do it this afternoon."

"I almost got it done," Riley said. "Jesus, it looks bad for those kids."

"Maybe they didn't do it," Deglin said.

Riley looked at him bleakly. "Maybe not," he said. "If he'd been shot or knifed, I'd know they didn't. But he was hit, so they could have, not meaning to. But that don't make him any less dead, I guess."

Deglin nodded and Riley looked back into his coffee cup for a minute before he lifted it to his mouth and drained it. He put it back on the counter and pushed it away.

"If they didn't do it, Mark," he said, "they're going to have a tough time proving it."

Deglin drank his own coffee and got off the stool.

Riley went on, fumbling in his pocket and pulling out a handful of change, "Those kids ain't got an alibi to bless them," and the dime tinkled on the marble counter.

Back at the station, they worked to finish the report. When it was done, Riley pushed the papers together in a stack and the carbons in another stack and clipped them together. They went together to Knight's office. There was a fat young man sitting opposite his desk and when they walked in the fat young man stopped talking and waited for them to leave.

"Everything here?" Knight asked, holding the reports and leafing through them quickly.

"Except the fingerprint reports," Riley said. "I called down but the phones were busy."

Knight nodded. "I got them. Phelps just called."

"Anything?" Deglin asked.

"Plenty."

They waited and Knight looked up, his mouth tight, deep lines in his heavy cheeks. "Most of them," he said, "were Paine's."

"How about those on the window?" Riley said.

Knight's glance was wintry. "Washington checked back. They belong to an ex-Army nurse, Morgan Taylor," he said.

He kept his eyes on them for a minute and Riley scowled. Deglin

NIGHT CRY

put his hand to his face and took it away quickly.

The fat young man spoke then. He had a deep businesslike voice. "The man, Redfield, probably ran out on her," he said.

Riley turned and regarded him as though he were an insect. "What are you talking about?"

The fat young man smiled calmly. "What you are. I'm Jeffries, out of the DA's office."

"This is Dan Riley, Jeffries," Knight said. "And Mark Deglin. They've been working on the case. Deglin just knocked off that Scalise thing, too."

"I've heard of the boys," Jeffries said. He was young, but he talked as if he were older than any of them, older even than Knight. He got to his feet. He had had his sharply pressed grey trouser legs pulled high, and now the cuffs fell perfectly so that they touched his highly polished shoes. "I'll take one of those copies," he said to Knight. "The DA and I are going over it at dinner. We'll probably work on it tonight. We want to move in on this one, inspector."

Knight nodded, his expression still wintry, his voice cold. "Yeah," he said. "This one will really be in the papers."

"That's right," Jeffries said, smiling and nodding. "The department's going to look good. It isn't often these tough ones are cracked this quickly."

"Yeah," Riley said. "The department's going to look great."

Deglin's hand went to his jaw again and came back quickly.

The day was drawing to a close, the factory was about to change shifts but they weren't done yet. There was one thing more to happen. Moments after Jeffries left, Clem Smith got into the office. He did not announce himself, because he knew that Knight probably would not talk to him. He pushed open the door and came in, his tall body slumped, his face more worn and filled with a look of deep humility. He looked at the three men and then, not resolutely, but with the appearance of one who has it coming to him and is ready to take it, he went to the window and half sat against the sill. No one greeted him.

"I guess it's the racket we're in," he said hesitantly.

It was not like Smith but it fitted him, the way he looked now.

"Yeah," Knight said. "I guess it is."

"Isn't much we can do," Smith said. "See what comes out."

"You can do something with the way you handle the story," Knight said sharply.

Smith shook his head. "There isn't much I can do about it now," he said. "There's no line on the girl yet. Morgan, I mean."

"No. But we'll get her."

"I'm aware of that," Smith said. "I mean, no line on whether she was actually a part of it."

Knight's voice was suddenly harder and colder than it had ever been. "I don't know about that," he said. "The DA's office makes the cases. We just find out what we can find out."

"I mean, you haven't found out anything else," Smith said quietly.

"So far as I know," Knight said, "there isn't any case. There's just an old lady and what she saw through a window on a foggy night. And there's—a body."

He paused and the silence was complete. For the moment, there were not even any ringing telephones or clacking typewriters or muffled voices from outside the office. There was just what an old lady had seen on a foggy night, and what a young girl and a young man had said, and what the people who had been at the gambling club had said about Paine—all that now with new significance— and a body.

"What do you think, Mark?" Smith asked.

"I just work here," Deglin said.

"I know," Smith said, nodding. "It's just the goddamn racket we're in."

15

It was hard to think, she decided. Hard to know what to do.

She sat quietly in the chair. Beside the bed, as in some hotel rooms, there was a combination night table and radio. She had turned it on earlier, while dressing for dinner, and then she had heard. Now music filled the room softly, strings and reeds and something by Gershwin. But soon, during the next news period, she would hear it again.

They had found Kendall Paine. She remembered him—his handsome, intent face, his sudden flashing smiles, his quick bitter anger. And now they had found him, murdered. And they had also found Pete Redfield and they were looking for Morgan Taylor.

It was hard to know what to do. She had stayed in New York the night before, registering late at the hotel because—well, because she and Pete had had dinner. She had bounced back vigorously from what she had felt had been Ken's deliberate dropping of her. But while she and Pete had had dinner and had danced and had laughed, Ken had been dead.

There was a picture in her mind that she could not erase. She could not know that it was not the proper picture. The proper one would have made her violently ill. In her picture, the water was clear and cold and green and his pale, wax-like face floated just beneath the surface, distorted slightly by occasional ripples, moving gently in the clean cold tide.

She put her hands to her face and held them there. The skin was dry and hot, as her eyes were dry and hot. She had not cried, nor did she feel like crying. She felt only an ache and emptiness and this inability to know what to do.

Could it have been Pete? Her thoughts twisted violently under the impact of it, as they had every time she allowed herself to whisper the words. But could it have been?

Then the music faded and the announcer began again. He said exactly the words he had an hour before, and he said them with the same degree of restrained excitement. "Today," he said, the excitement withheld but present, "what had started as a routine search for missing Kendall Paine deepened into one of New York's most tragic mysteries. The body of Kendall Paine, war hero, writer, remembered by all America as one of the country's outstanding football players, was found sunk in a tugboat slip, wrapped in a blanket from his own bed, weighted down by sashweights taken from his own window."

She took her hands from her face. She heard her name and that of Pete Redfield, and the word that the police department had mobilized for a quick solution to the tragedy, and the immediate impress of justice.

Then it was Pete, she thought with sick certainty. Big, quiet Pete, who had smiled when Kendall Paine had first come along—had seen Ken and Morgan laugh together, how their eyes lighted together, and had smiled and done nothing except get a little drunker than usual once in a while, and maybe smack Paine when he was out of line. He couldn't have meant it. He didn't mean nasty or terrible things. It couldn't have been Pete.

She went to the bedside table, suddenly, Then her hand stayed as she was about to take the telephone, and she sank down on the bed.

She had thought of Deglin, but she knew she couldn't go to the station. She wanted to talk to Deglin, just to Deglin. Curiously, just the thought of his dark, attentive eyes, the hard competent lines of his face, gave her a feeling of relief.

But she couldn't talk to him there. There, all the voices in the world would come at her, inquiring, unbelieving, cold, merciless. Nor could she run. The dog waits for the cat, the cat waits for the mouse, and the police wait. She remembered Deglin's words. She could not run.

It was hard to think, to know what do to.

The man who sat opposite Knight was pale and drawn. He held one hand in the other in his lap and he kneaded it slowly, but only that betrayed his nervousness and anxiety.

"We have no knowledge at all that your daughter is involved in this by any more than her friendship with both Paine and Redfield,"

NIGHT CRY 135

Knight was saying.

Mr. Taylor nodded his grey head.

"Thank you," he said. "I needed some assurance. That's why I was anxious to talk to you."

"I'm glad you did," Knight said. He regarded Taylor soberly for a long minute. "Mr. Taylor, do you know what time your daughter arrived home two nights ago?"

"Why?"

"It may have some bearing."

"Then you'll forgive me if I don't answer it?"

Knight nodded. "We'll find out," he said.

"I'm aware of that," Taylor agreed. His voice was a little husky and he seemed suddenly quite tired. "However, I intend that Morgan shall have every chance for a proper defense and I intend to engage the best lawyer in the country to see that she gets it. Until then, I judge it best to keep my own counsel."

Knight nodded.

"Thank you for coming in," he said.

Knight found Deglin and Riley down at the desk, watching the teletype. Riley looked up as he came in and went back to an elaborate doodle he was working on in his notebook. It had curves and straight lines and shaded areas until virtually the whole page had been covered. He had been at it for quite a time.

"She's probably gone to a hotel," Knight said. "She wouldn't know how to hide."

"We've started a hotel check," Deglin said.

Riley examined the page, found a place not entirely interlined and shaded and went to work on it.

"We got two reports already. Beauty shop operators. She's had her hair dyed two different colors according to them."

"She won't dye her hair," Knight said. "She won't do anything. She'll get scared and she'll go home."

"You've covered that," Deglin said.

Knight watched Riley complete the doodle. "Yeah, it's covered," he said. "You guys want to have dinner with me?"

Riley took the sheet of paper out of his notebook and wadded it up. He tossed it at a wastebasket and it missed and rolled across the floor. He sighed and went across to retrieve it and put it in the basket.

"I thought I'd go home, chief, if you don't mind. I'm bushed."

"You, Mark?"

Deglin's hand was at the muscle in his jaw. He took it away. "All right," he said.

They went to a small saloon on a side street between Sixth and Times Square, walking through the chill night, their heads bent against the wind. When they entered, Knight went directly to the long mahogany bar. Deglin followed him. A thin blondish man at the end of the bar saw them and left his place to come over.

"Hello, Al. Mark," he said. "That's a beaut you guys uncovered today."

Knight nodded. "Whisky," he said to the bartender, and Deglin said, "Make it two. Doubles." Then Knight turned to the blondish man and grimaced.

"Don't run into anything like it often," he said. "Thank God."

"The guy do it?"

Knight shrugged. "Looks that way, Matty."

The blondish head wagged. "You never can tell. I had to be over in the cells today. Looked in on him. Nice looking guy."

"Nice guy, too," Knight said. "That right, Mark?"

Deglin nodded without saying anything.

"Any line on the girl?"

"No," Knight said. "But we'll find her."

Matty nodded and went back to his end of the bar and Deglin watched him talk to men beside him, and the men look at Knight and himself, interest in their eyes.

They had another drink, and ordered their dinners from menus a waiter brought to the bar for them. When the waiter came back and said everything was ready, they took their third drinks to the table.

Deglin was feeling his. They made him morose, but he had stopped doing any thinking at all, and he was grateful for that. Knight looked at the steak in front of him, cut into it, and put a piece of the red dripping meat in his mouth. He chewed, swallowed, and looked at Deglin.

"Damned if I got much appetite, Mark," he said.

"I know," Deglin said.

NIGHT CRY

"At least you're managing to eat yours," Knight said.

Deglin looked at his plate and his steak was already half gone. He was not conscious of any feeling of hunger or of the pleasure of satisfying hunger. But the food was going and he put another piece of steak in his mouth and, chewing it, cut off still another.

"I'll bet I have insomnia tonight," Knight said reflectively.

"Why don't you knock yourself out with sleeping pills?" Deglin said.

"Sleeping pills?" Knight's disgust was enormous. "Those are for dames."

"Maybe," Deglin said. "But they do get you some rest."

Knight finally ate, slowly and methodically, so that Deglin was through with his coffee by the time Knight was ready for his. Deglin waited, impatience growing slowly while Knight sipped. At length they got up and paid their checks.

"Going back?" Knight said.

Deglin looked indecisive. He didn't want to. He knew that he would be unable to stand the intermittent stream of reports, inconclusive in themselves, proving only that somewhere in the city a lovely girl was sitting alone, wondering what to do, frightened of doing anything. She's heard by this time, he thought. By this time, she knows.

"I'm kind of tired, Al," he said.

Knight scowled. "Maybe I won't, either," he said. "Just a minute."

He turned to a phone booth, pulled open the door and went in. The door closed behind him and the light went on and Deglin watched him take money from his pocket and push it around in the palm of his hand, looking for a nickel. Finally he found one, put the rest of the money back, dialed, and waited. His voice rumbled and then he listened, nodding. When he came out, his expression was grave.

"Well, I guess I'd better go on over," he said.

"Something up?" Deglin asked.

Knight nodded. "They got a line on her. She'd registered in a hotel last night, under her own name. Left just before we started the register check. Maybe she's started to run."

Deglin's mouth worked and the muscle in his cheek moved spasmodically.

"I'll go over with you, Al," he said.

When they returned to the station, there was nothing more than that and little more they could do. They waited downstairs at the teletype for a while but it carried only routine messages. Then, as Smith came in from the small office which the newspapers kept on the corner across the street, Knight turned and went heavily up the marble stairs. Deglin waited for a minute, still watching the messages as they appeared on the paper, then followed. Smith went with him.

"I'll bet that poor kid is scared to death," he said as they climbed the stairs.

Deglin said nothing.

They went into Knight's outer office. Knight had his door closed and his voice rumbled behind the panel, its pauses marking the fact that he was on the phone. Instead of pushing the door open, Deglin went to one of the desks and sat down.

Smith looked at him closely with his bored, tired eyes.

"I haven't phoned in my story yet," he said.

Deglin nodded.

"They're probably going nuts. I can see old MacIntosh. He's going crazy." Smith's smile was small and tight. "But I can't. I'll be damned if I can."

"It's there," Deglin said.

"Do you believe it, Mark?" Smith asked.

Deglin leaned back in the chair and looked at Smith. "What do you want me to do?"

"You're a guy who knows about these things," Smith went on. "Am I nuts when I refuse to accept the fact that a couple of kids like that could have done a thing like that? It's never bothered me before. I've put the arm on murderers, hung them gladly a hundred times, even said to myself proudly, 'Look, you fine and able newspaperman, you most excellent journalist, so-and-so is frying at this minute because you wouldn't stay off the backs of those cement heads in the DA's office. You kept after them, badgered them, until now society is once again being protected and you are the finest existing example of the inspired journalist.'" He looked at Deglin for a minute. Then he added quietly, "I don't feel like that now, Mark. I feel like a bum."

NIGHT CRY   **139**

"What should I do?" Deglin said, his voice sharper.

"Don't you feel that way?"

"No," Deglin said.

Smith shook his head.

"I'm a cop," Deglin said.

"I talked to Redfield," Smith went on after a minute. "Yesterday, after the story had run. He was going to punch me in the nose, but he didn't."

"What did he do?"

"Nothing. But that's not the point. I don't think that he would have handled it the way it looks. I think he would have done this: he would have punched Paine and when he saw that Paine was dead he'd go to somebody and he'd say, 'Look here, I whacked this guy and I did it too hard. Now I don't know what to do about it.'"

"Maybe he did," Deglin said.

"What do you mean by that?" Smith said sharply.

"I don't know yet what I mean. I don't know much about it yet," Deglin said. "I've gotta wait until we can see what we've got. There's nothing else we can do."

"Yes, there is," Smith said softly. "You can find out who did it."

Deglin was silent and Smith watched him.

"You can," he went on. "Someone did it. I don't think it was them. I don't see how it could have been. You could try to find out."

Deglin closed his eyes. "It's not the work for one man," he said. "It's the work for a whole force. We get what we can, and when it's tied together we see what the pattern is."

"But isn't there something else?" Smith asked desperately. "One little thing that throws it another way? You've got to have something. It would help the story."

"You're getting worried too fast," Deglin said. "The DA has everything we know. He hasn't had any presentment yet. He doesn't even know himself what he's going to do until everything is in."

"The hell—" Smith began bitterly, then Knight's door opened and Knight came out.

"Not much more we can do tonight, Mark," he said.

"Okay," Deglin said. He got out of the chair and went out of the room without saying good-by to either Knight or Smith.

He took the subway uptown and got off at the stop nearest his apartment building. He walked across to the East River in the cold whipping wind, head down, hands in his topcoat pockets. His mind was numbed and drugged, as though refusing to have anything to do with events.

When he let himself into his apartment he walked through the dark living room into his bedroom and dropped on the bed. He took off his hat and lay there, staring up into the darkness. He could feel the muscle in his face working and he put his hand on it. It was strange and alive under his fingers. Like his own mind, it seemed to have no relationship to the rest of him, moving of its own accord, independent of his wishes. Then suddenly, it was annoying and maddening. He lay on the bed, his hands clenched, the perspiration starting on his face.

When he could stand it no longer, he got to his feet and went blindly to the kitchen, hitting the door violently with his shoulder so that he half spun in the darkness. He fumbled in the cabinet above the sink and found a squat bottle of Scotch. He took it with him to the living room, feeling for a light, finding it, flipping the switch so that the soft glow filled a corner of the room.

He took off his topcoat and dropped it across the back of a chair, then carried the bottle with him to one of the big chairs near the fireplace. His hands shook a little as he pulled the cork out, and the fiery liquor burned his throat sharply. He sat with the bottle between his knees. He didn't take another drink, but the feel of the bottle, smooth and cool in his hands, was a strange relief.

He had no idea how long he had sat, staring unseeingly in front of him, when the chimes rang softly. He put the bottle on the table and went to the door.

She hadn't dyed her hair two different shades in two different beauty shops. Except that her eyes were larger in her pale face, she was the same as she had been, straight and lovely, her dark hair shining in the light of the foyer.

"I had to see you, Mr. Deglin," she said quickly.

Deglin stood aside, against the wall, holding the door. "Come on in," he said.

He stood straight and tense, watching her go past him. She had done what shouldn't have been done—and her coming, not frightened or terror-stricken, but seeking—had done what nothing else could do. The barriers that had held his emotions broke and thoughts came flooding at him, released. They had escaped and now they would burrow and work, reappearing briefly and scuttlingly, like rats in an alley. They were doing it already—the gagging, snoring breaths of Kendall Paine; the soughing cry of the wind and rain on the waterfront, and the hissing bubbles of the water, lost in the creaking of the tugs at their moorings; the whipping fog and the slowly moving, grey-haired conductor taking his ticket, looking at the bandage on his eye.

He went across to her. "A drink?"

"Please," she said.

He went to the kitchen and got two glasses and brought them back with a tray of ice and a pitcher of water. He made a drink slowly and handed it to her. He didn't have one.

"I found your name in the telephone book," she said. "I've been here twice. I—I thought you weren't coming home."

"I've been here a while," Deglin said.

"I went for a walk." She smiled tremulously. "I do quite a bit of walking."

She tasted her drink, and Deglin watched her, not knowing what to say. When she lifted her eyes to him again, they were suddenly filled with her torture. She started to say something but her voice lost itself in a sob, and she sat for a moment, her face lifted to Deglin, tears welling in her eyes.

"I don't know what to do," she said.

Deglin nodded, wordlessly.

"Do they think it was Pete? Do they think he did it?"

"They don't know what to think, yet," Deglin said. He felt his hands clenching and unclenching at his sides and he quieted them with an effort.

"But they do."

She looked at him, knowing, and he nodded.

"He couldn't have," she said softly. "Isn't there something you can do?"

"He can't account for his time," Deglin said. "He says he was in his room and he sticks to that. But no one saw him. No one heard him in the room."

"You've asked?" she said.

"I haven't," Deglin said. "But it has been checked. Others checked it."

She was silent for a long moment. Then she said, looking at the drink in her hand, "Years ago, when I was a little girl, I used to wake sometimes in the night. I'd lie in bed, and hear the far-away cries of the hunting things in the woods and they'd fill me with a kind of a lonesomeness and terror for the creatures that were being hunted in the darkness. I—" She paused. "I'd forgotten how I used to feel then," she ended softly.

Deglin stilled his clenching hands again.

"I'll try to help," he said. He made himself a drink and lit a cigarette and sat down in the chair opposite her. He sat for a minute, tensely, looking at her, not saying anything, the end of the cigarette threading itself off into a sudden grey mushroom of smoke.

"If you can prove where you were and when, after you left Paine's place the first time," he said.

Her voice was a whisper. "Is—is that when he was killed?"

Deglin nodded.

"Then he didn't go to Greenwich at all?"

"That's right."

"But—"

"It was someone in his clothes."

He watched her take it—watched the horror grow in her face as what little color she had faded.

"You didn't see Pete Redfield at all that night?"

She nodded.

"When?"

"In the evening. Very early. Ken and I had had dinner uptown. Pete was in the restaurant."

"Did you talk?"

"Not very long. Ken wanted him to go with us to the gambling club. Pete wouldn't."

"Did they argue?"

She said nothing, her face lowered, her hands still. They waited in the silence and Deglin's glass made a noise as he lifted it to his lips and drank and put it back on the table beside the bottle and the pitcher.

"How long were you in Paine's room? After you came back from

NIGHT CRY 143

the gambling club?"

"Not long. Only a few minutes."

"Not when Redfield was there?"

She was puzzled by the question. "I hadn't even known he had been there until he told me the next night."

"Were you at the window? The window in the back of the room?" Deglin's voice was rough, his mouth worked while he waited for her answer.

She frowned with thought. "Why?" she said.

"Were you there?"

She nodded.

"Why were you at the window?" he said.

She paused for a long space, and when she spoke, her voice was very low. "There's a tree there. Ken and I had watched it all through the Spring. It was as if it was our tree."

"Yes," Deglin said.

"I was looking at it," she said. "The light from the window fell on it, and it seemed as though it was dying. I just looked at it."

"And then you went out and walked in the rain."

She nodded.

"You didn't see anyone, or stop any place when you were walking?"

"No, I didn't."

"The police know that you came back to Paine's long after the one o'clock train had left for Greenwich," Deglin said.

She started a protest, but it died on her lips. "Do they?" she said.

Deglin's tension mounted. He could feel it shaking him. "You didn't see anyone while you were walking? You didn't stop any place?"

She shook her head. "I don't think so. I don't remember." There was a hopelessness in her voice. "I try to recall what I did, but it escapes me."

Deglin leaned forward in his chair. "Do you think that if we—you and I—walked where you went, you might recall something?"

"That's important?" she asked.

Deglin nodded. "Maybe if we can't find who did do it, we can prove you had nothing to do with it."

"I'll try," she said. She was suddenly relieved. "You do want to help, don't you?"

"Yes," Deglin said. He had wanted to say, look, baby, this wasn't planned to hurt anyone. It was planned to be just a guy going away someplace, and staying there long enough to be forgotten. But he said yes again, and got to his feet and went looking for his topcoat and hat. When he got back, he took Morgan's arm and they went together to the elevator.

Downstairs, waiting for a cab, she said hopefully, "Maybe you could talk to Pete, too. Maybe there is something he could remember."

"We'll do this first," Deglin said.

The cab took them through the misting rain and the empty streets. They said nothing. In the faint light that illuminated the back of the cab, Deglin's face was intent, his eyes guarded. Morgan sat thoughtfully in the corner, her face turning occasionally to the clouded windows of the cab. Deglin leaned forward in his seat to direct the driver for the final few blocks, and when they finally pulled up before the building in which Paine had had his room, he said to Morgan, "We'll get wet. Do you think we could follow your steps with the cab?"

"I don't know," she said.

"We'll not try it," Deglin decided, and he paid the driver and opened the door and helped her out.

For a moment, she stood silently, thinking; then she turned. and with Deglin at her side, moved through the rain toward the corner.

"I stopped at a place for cigarettes. If I can remember it," she said.

"That may help," Deglin said.

They walked, and twice she stopped before tiny candy stores looking at them with indecision. Finally she turned into one. There was a bent, elderly man behind a tiny marble fountain. He was reading a paper. When he heard the door close behind them, he looked up.

Morgan smiled at him.

"Hello," she said.

He smiled back.

"Do you remember me coming in here the other night? About a week ago?"

"For cigarettes," the elderly man said, nodding. He started to

NIGHT CRY

move toward the cigarette racks, and Deglin named a brand and put change on the counter.

"You got a good memory," he said, smiling.

The elderly man laughed. "Ain't got many customers," he said. "Not that late."

"Thanks," Deglin said. He picked up the cigarettes and took Morgan's arm and went out the door with her.

"But maybe he could tell more," she said.

"That's enough for now," Deglin said. "We can come back to him."

"Oh," she said.

"We'll have to find others," Deglin said. "You walked for a long while. You could have gone right back from here. We have to establish that you were just wandering around, without a plan. Establish a reasonable doubt that you did anything else."

They walked silently, side by side, in the rain, across to the Village, and through the lonesome side streets that move like the interlinings of a jigsaw puzzle. At Washington Square, they turned, and halfway through the vast empty block, Morgan stopped suddenly.

"I think I remember something," she said.

"What?" Deglin asked.

"I was going to sit down here but the benches were wet and it had started to rain harder. I went across to Eighth Street and down to Sixth Avenue. There were people there."

"They wouldn't remember," Deglin said. "We couldn't find them anyway."

"No," she said. "Wait. There was a newsstand, with an overhang. And it began raining so hard that I stood under that. There was a newsman there. I stood there for quite a while. I didn't notice him but he should remember me."

"Good," Deglin said.

They turned back to Fifth Avenue, walking hurriedly, and went down Eighth Street. While still yards away from the newsstand, Morgan said, "That's it. That's the man, too. I remember, he said, 'Good evening.'"

She hurried ahead of Deglin then, and he saw her go up to the newsdealer, her face smiling. But she stopped short and said nothing to him. By the time Deglin reached her, she had turned and was waiting for him wordlessly. The newsdealer was standing politely, his sightless eyes turned toward her, his hand on the pile of morning tabloids.

Deglin took her arm and they moved down the street.

"That's all," she said softly. "That's all I remember. I waited here for a while, then I walked some more and went back."

"You didn't stop at a—" Deglin started. Then he took her arm and stopped her slow steps. They waited together while the uniformed cop got out of the patrol car parked at the curb and came toward them.

He was big and quite polite.

"Are you Morgan Taylor?" he said, looking at her and at Deglin. She nodded. "Yes," she said in a small voice.

She turned her face to Deglin. He was reaching into his pocket. He took out his badge and showed it to the patrolman. "This is under control, officer," he said.

The officer looked at it and turned to the patrol car and nodded at the cop who sat at the opened window. "We've got a call on Miss Taylor, Lieutenant," he said.

"I know."

"Is there anything we can do?"

"No, thanks," Deglin said.

He watched impassively as the patrolman went back to the black-and-white car and it moved slowly away from the curb.

"I should have watched that," he said harshly. He turned to her. "We'll have to do something," he said.

"Do something?"

"They'll check in with the Telegraph Bureau." He rubbed his hand against his cheek savagely. "There isn't much time."

"But there's nothing to do," she said. "They know I'm with you. It would just make trouble for you."

She saw the agonized planes of his face and the spasmodic working of the muscle in his cheek. She put a hand on his arm.

"It's all right," she said. "I don't mind. I would like to go home tonight. I promise I'll come in in the morning."

When Deglin got back to his apartment, he took off his topcoat and his hat and his jacket and went to a chair by the fireplace and

NIGHT CRY 147

sat down. After a while, he took the bottle from the table and held it in his hands. He looked at it and poured a drink, and set the bottle back on the little cabinet again. He sat there most of the night, the light over the chair glowing, the bottle glinting softly amber.

16

Deglin was haggard when he got in the next morning, but no more so than Knight. The captain's face was grey and his eyes were red-rimmed. Only Riley looked as though he had slept well, but he remained quiet and thoughtful.

Knight and Riley were already in Knight's office, Riley at the window sill, when Deglin walked in, and Knight said at once:

"She's on her way in. Where did you find her?"

Deglin sat down. "One of those things," he said.

"You talked to her?"

"A little," Deglin said. "Not much. Not enough to mean anything."

Knight looked at him fretfully. "I guess she'll talk, huh? We'll probably be writing this one off."

Riley spoke for the first time. "I'd like to get on a case where I could beat the hell out of somebody and know they deserve it. It'd make me feel better."

Knight fell to drumming the desk with his fingers.

"Look, Mark," he said. "What were you doing with the girl downtown."

"Checking some stuff."

Knight leaned forward. "Well, what about it, dammit. Did you get anything? Had anyone seen her?"

Deglin shook his head. "Nothing that would do any good. She had just walked around."

"Okay," Knight said. His fingers drummed some more and he went on, "I got some work I can do."

Deglin started to get up out of the chair he had taken, but Knight shook his head. "No need to go, Mark," he said. "We're just waiting for Jeffries of the DA's office. You guys won't bother me."

They sat while Knight went slowly through the pile of paper work on his desk.

"We got anonymous letters about this thing already," he said once. Another time he said—and there was disgust in his voice—"We're

NIGHT CRY

going to have to do more on this Spieler case. He'll wiggle out, sure as hell."

The minutes wore on and the papers rattled crisply as he turned them in their folders. Finally the door opened and Jeffries walked in, his round figure immaculate, his round face fresh and business-like. He had a look of exactness and an air of bustle and efficiency— a bright young businessman excited with the well-oiled smoothness of his work.

"Hello, Captain," he said genially, smiling. Knight nodded and watched him hang up his topcoat on a never-used hanger and put his hat over the hook. He came across the room, bobbing his head sharply at Riley at the window and Deglin in the chair. Riley looked bored. Jeffries sat in the chair opposite Knight. He unstrapped his briefcase and set it on the creases of his pants. Then he put an elbow on it and spoke to Knight.

"Well, Captain," he said, "we've been through your reports. An excellent job, the boss says. It would be nice if we could have some additional information but I know what your department is up against on a case like this."

"Thanks," Knight said dryly.

"You've done a surprisingly good job." Jeffries opened the briefcase and took from it the folder of reports. "First," he said, "we've tried to talk to Redfield." He shook his head. "He is adamant. Second, we understand the girl is on her way in. We'll want to talk to her."

Knight nodded, waiting.

"Now," Jeffries said, leaning forward, "here's a pattern we've made out of the information we have. We want to see what you think of it. It's circumstantial, of course, and were worried about what they can do to the old woman once they get her on the stand."

"What's the case?" Knight said heavily.

Jeffries leaned forward further and looked earnestly at Knight. "Now this makes good sense," he said. "The girl had been Redfield's girl. We know that, and we can also prove that Paine took her away from him and that, on at least one occasion, Redfield and Paine have fought. At no time, probably, did Redfield ever hit Paine any harder than Paine was hit when he was killed. That was a broken neck, incidentally. You knew that?"

Knight nodded.

"Well, Paine calls Redfield, asking to borrow money. Redfield comes to Paine's room. This Taylor girl is still there. She and Paine have been arguing. Redfield still loves the girl, understand, and sees that they have been fighting. His instinctive reaction is to defend the girl. He does it by hitting Paine, which he has done before. Only this time he kills him."

He looked at them and they said nothing and he said, "So far so good? They're frightened, of course, the minute they find Paine is dead. Redfield gets into Paine's clothes and goes off to lay a false trail of his departure. In the meanwhile, the girl goes out to get wire so that they can dispose of the body. Redfield could get into Paine's clothes all right. It'd be a tight fit, maybe, but he could do it. But after he has laid the trail he runs out on the girl. She returns to the room, waits for him. He doesn't come, and after a while she finally realizes that she must dispose of the body herself. And she does it."

He stopped and looked at each of the men in turn, awaiting their reactions. He smiled faintly in anticipation.

"For Christ's sake," Riley said. "How could she have carried the guy? Don't be nuts."

Jeffries' smile broadened slightly. He dug into his briefcase and brought out a photograph, which he looked at for a moment before he handed it across to Knight.

"Here," he said.

Knight looked at it for a long minute, and then, wordlessly, handed it across to Riley. Riley glanced at it briefly, then came away from the window to give it to Deglin. Deglin looked at it. It was a war department photograph, which had been released in the general news pool following the bombardment of an American hospital. The picture was one of despair and horror. Most of the figures were lost in the smoke and rubble of the hospital, but not lost, clear in the foreground, was Morgan Taylor, carrying a wounded man. Her face was strained and agonized and dirty, and she was looking directly at the camera.

"There are a couple of things we can check on," Jeffries aid.

Riley took his notebook out and held it ready.

Deglin watched Jeffries' manicured, efficient hands as they sorted the papers in the briefcase. Riley believes it, he thought, as Knight

NIGHT CRY

does and as I appear to. Riley, and soon everyone else—wherever there are wires to carry news and photographs and newspapers to print them, news announcers and radios to carry the measured excitement of their voices. It's being tried now, and they are it.

Riley's pencil scratched in the notebook. "The wire may have been new," Jeffries was saying, "but we ought to run a check on it."

"Lab job," Riley said.

"And how about the attendant at the ferry? She had to go right by there."

Riley's pencil scratched. "We'll try him. It was foggy, though."

"Certainly," Jeffries said sharply. "We know it was foggy. But there may have been a break in the fog. The man may have gone for a walk. Anything may have happened. The other thing is that kitbag—Paine's bag. If you can find where Redfield hid it, we're in. Try his room, check rooms, friends, what have you. You'll put plenty of manpower on this."

"Plenty," Knight said.

Jeffries' head bobbed. He glanced through his sheets of paper, his mouth pursed. "Well," he said, "I guess that's it. The whole theory may be knocked into a cocked hat, of course, but it's the most logical right now. And there's always the chance that either or both of them might break. Particularly her, if we're right and he ran out on her."

He put the papers back and buckled the straps of the briefcase. Then he got his coat, shrugged into it, and set his hat carefully on his head. "Guess we're in for a little more nasty weather," he said conversationally, peering out the window.

"Yeah," Knight said.

Morgan came in with her father a half-hour later. Smith was with her, too. He had her by the arm as they came through the door of Knight's office and he looked belligerently at Knight and said, "I'm staying with her."

Knight looked at him coldly. For an instant, it appeared as though he was about to have Smith thrown out. Then he shrugged.

Deglin had risen to his feet and moved over to the door. He nodded at Morgan's tremulous smile. Riley said, gravely, "Hello, Miss Taylor."

"You know," Knight said, looking first at the girl and then at her father, "that what you tell me will go into the records."

"I know," she said.

Her father came forward to the desk and put his hand on it. "Morgan has insisted that she come in like this. I explained it was not necessary—that she should move only with proper counsel."

"Please, Dad," she said. She looked at Knight and her face was soft and hurt and pleading. "You think Pete Redfield did it," she said.

Knight made no move. He watched her, his big body slack and waiting.

"He couldn't have," she said. "He's not like that. It was someone else, someone terrible."

"Can you tell us exactly what your moves were that night? Exactly what you did, step by step, from the first time you saw Kendall Paine until you finally took the train back to Greenwich?"

She was silent for a moment, controlling herself. "Yes, sir," she said finally in a tiny voice.

Riley nodded, getting out his notebook again, and her eyes went to it. She began to speak, her voice hesitant. Smith looked from Knight to Riley, and then back to the door where Deglin stood. Deglin was watching the girl intently. His hands flexed at his side. His mouth was a thin, flat line in his dark face. He seemed fascinated by the girl and by her soft words, almost mesmerized, so that he was not aware of Smith's steady regard. Finally, with almost an effort, his eyes moved from the half-profile of her face to Knight, sitting squarely in his chair. Knight listened and nodded occasionally.

He said, after a bit, interrupting her, "Paine borrowed money from you. Why did he call Redfield?"

"He returned it to me," she said. "When they—" the pause was a breath while she looked for the word "—asked us to leave the club, they cashed his chips and he returned the money."

"I see," Knight said, and fell silent again, ponderous and impersonal behind the desk.

"Did he ask you to return to his room with him?" he said finally.

"No," she said. "No. I wanted to go. I wanted to talk to him."

"What did you talk about?"

"Him. Us."

"You had a fight?"

NIGHT CRY 153

She nodded, miserably.

"How long were you there?"

"I don't know. Only a few minutes."

"What did you do while you were there? Exactly, what did you do?"

She put her hands to her face for the first time and there was a world of weariness in the gesture. "It's hard to remember," she explained, her voice shaking suddenly. "I tried to talk to him about the way things were going, but he wouldn't let me. He had a drink, and after I tried to tell him that he would have to change or he would spoil everything he had hoped for and I had hoped for, then he told me—" she stopped.

"Yes?" Knight said.

"That I— I could never understand him, that things were impossible."

"And you left then?"

"Yes."

He watched her, his eyes still impersonal, his expression still noncommittal.

"You saw no one while you walked? You didn't stop in for coffee or a drink? You didn't call anyone?"

"No," she said. "I didn't."

"And when you came back? Why did you come back?"

"I'd made up my mind," she said faintly.

"About what?"

"About us."

"What?"

She flushed. "That maybe I was being unfair. That maybe Ken did need understanding and help."

"You were going to tell him that?"

"Yes," she said simply.

Knight rubbed his mouth. "Miss Taylor, there is a window at the back of Paine's room. Were you at that window for any reason?"

The question came to her eyes again. "Yes," she said, and the question was in the word, too.

"Why?" Knight asked.

Her eyes went to Deglin. "I— I was watching a tree," she said.

And Smith, who had been watching the girl, saw Deglin move,

open the door beside him, and step out. Smith watched the door, hearing her quiet words, and Knight's short questions, waiting for it to open and for Deglin to reappear. When the minutes passed, and Deglin did not come, Smith looked first at Riley, who was bent over the notebook, then at Knight. He got to his feet and went to the door and out of the room.

17

Out of the confusion of Deglin's thoughts, one grew steadily clearer.

He could feel his fascination with Morgan Taylor. It enveloped him in a soft, powerful embrace, so that he was unable to stop looking at her. Her words, spoken softly, made their imprint on his mind almost unnoticed.

He had watched her clear, pure profile, the way her eyes lowered and lifted, the movements of her body in the chair, the sudden trembling of her pale hands.

What he had heard—what she had said—was the truth. Just as the words Pete Redfield kept doggedly repeating were the truth. It was inconceivable that someone like Morgan, lovely and cleared-eyed and sweet, should be touched by even so much as the edge of violent death. Both Knight and Riley had felt that impossibility. Their awareness of it had sobered them, made them hate the job that made it necessary for them first to contemplate, then slowly to accept it as possibility.

But because the few facts they did know incontrovertibly—and the one shrieking fact of Paine's death—had formed an illusion of truth, the actual truth was pale and weak. It could not stand up before the illusion.

He had managed to take his eyes from her and look at Knight. Knight, solid and unmoving, was not believing her. He was hearing what had happened, exactly as it had happened, and yet he was becoming more coldly unbelieving as her simple words went on. Some of it was beginning to show in his brief questions. Not in the questions themselves, so much as in the way he spoke them. Enough so that Morgan was beginning to feel it. It was growingly apparent in the softness of her voice, the trembling of it, that she too was beginning to think of the truth she spoke as an illusion, to doubt the actuality of the things she told.

"Why?" Knight had asked bluntly.

Deglin had watched her lovely profile turn and had seen her eyes full on him, pleading, asking. She had said, very softly, "I— I was watching a tree."

She had looked at him for another instant, then turned back to Knight. Deglin had pulled open the door and stepped out of the room.

He went across the corridor to the detectives' waiting room and sat at a desk, his hands on the dark, metal-edged composition top, his head lowered. He frowned in thought so deep that when someone came by and said, "Hello, Mark," he did not look up.

The man went on by and out of the room, his heavy footsteps fading in the corridor, and still Deglin sat. Finally, he shook his head sharply, as though to clear his mind, and opened a drawer in the desk and took from it the folder on Paine. He went through it carefully, looking for anything that might previously have been overlooked, anything that Redfield might have said to Jeffries or Morgan might have said to Riley or anyone else. When he had finished, he put the folder back again. It was there, in black-and-white in a blue folder, the monumental untruth.

He got up from the desk, his head still bent. Then he turned and went out of the building. He was nervous again, as he had been when he had walked to meet Izzie. And he needed a drink. The palms of his hands were wet, and the wind-whipped rain that had begun to fall mixed with the beads of sweat that formed on his forehead and cheeks and ran together to his chin. His back was cold. So was the pit of his stomach.

He went around the corner to the first saloon. It was long and narrow, with a long bar down the left, and a string of narrow booths down the right. It was quiet and empty. A huge jukebox at the rear looked forlorn and dark in the gloom and the one oval, orange neon beer sign that sputtered in the window accentuated the murkiness of the street outside.

Deglin went over to the bar, to the exact middle of it, and the bartender who had been standing at the end came over to him, nodding in an inquiring way.

"Double whisky," Deglin said.

"Soda?"

"Neat."

NIGHT CRY

He watched the whisky push itself up the sides of the glass. When the bartender stopped pouring the thin red stream, Deglin picked up the glass, shaking a little, and drank. His cold stomach burned at once, comfortably. The shaking quieted.

"Another," he said, his voice thin from the burning of the whisky in his throat.

He drank that one, too, and motioned to the man to pour another.

"Lousy day," the bartender said.

"Shut up," Deglin said, watching the whisky come up in the glass.

When the whisky had stopped, he raised his head and looked evenly at the bartender. The bartender walked down beside the line of evenly stacked glasses, leaving Deglin's vision; and Deglin saw himself in the back-bar mirror. He looked at himself until he stopped seeing himself in the mirror at all, but rather saw things as they must now develop. He saw and felt and heard the long, careful checking with the DA's office as the case was readied . . . the pleasant interviews with the little old lady, Mr. Jeffries nice as pie . . . the quiet buzz of the court room . . . Morgan's pale face beside the composed face of the police matron . . . Pete Redfield, belligerent and confused, listening as the state's truth was unfolded, smashing and tearing their own truths . . . Riley's quiet testimony about the sash cords, his own firm testimony....

"You then went to Redfield's rooms, Mr. Deglin?"

"Yes, sir," he would answer.

"Why did you go, please?"

"A Mr. Jeffries had suggested that we try to find Paine's kitbag."

"Mr. Jeffries?"

"He's with the District Attorney's office."

"So you went to Mr. Redfield's room, thinking it might be there?"

"Yes, sir. There was a chance it would be."

"You entered his room and discovered it."

"I discovered a kitbag. Yes, sir."

"Is this the bag you found in Mr. Redfield's room?"

(PAUSE) "Yes, sir. It is."

"The state offers this in evidence. A kitbag stenciled with the name of the deceased and his Army serial number."

The excited murmur of the crowd . . . and the drone of the bailiff's voice. The hopeless terror in Morgan Taylor's eyes . . . and in Pete

Redfield's the quick-flaring anger that fades almost as soon as it has come....

Deglin shook his head sharply and lowered his eyes to the dark mahogany of the bar. His drink glittered dully at his hand. He lifted it and drank, letting it run down his throat slowly.

He let his mind play with the thought. The kitbag! It was the one final thing that could solidify the illusion into truth, pale truth to illusion. It would require finesse: getting the bag, taking it to Redfield's, finding it there, and calling the landlady to show her the kitbag, to ask if she had seen it before. Her truth that she had not would in the face of the kitbag itself become illusion.

And suddenly, the sickness rose overpoweringly in Deglin. He saw quickly, and with startling clarity, the picture of Izzie, helpless in the shadows of the areaway, his gun useless at his side. He heard again his sobbing curses in the night. And blending with them, a crazy fugue, the lonesome crying sounds of the hunter and the hunted in the night.

And he was sick. He turned from the bar and found the restroom. He stood at the washbasin, his head down, fighting the waves of nausea. When they had quieted, he ran the cold water and took up handfuls of it and put it against his eyes. Then he dried his face and went back to the bar.

He stood at the bar and looked down at the bartender who ignored him.

"Say," Deglin said.

The bartender looked up the long line of mahogany at him. He started slowly over and when he got to Deglin's place, he said nothing.

"I'm sorry about jumping on you," Deglin said.

The bartender nodded.

Deglin got his badge out and showed it to him. "Been on a tough one," he said.

The bartender's manner changed slightly.

"I want you to do something for me," Deglin said.

He dug out his wallet with careful movements and pulled the storage receipt out of it.

"Got an envelope?" he said.

The bartender hesitated. "Well—" he began.

NIGHT CRY   **159**

"Good God," Deglin said. "I don't have to give you a tip to do this, do I?"

The bartender hesitated again. "You at Fifty-fourth Street?"

"Yeah," Deglin said.

The bartender went back down and dug around under the bar for a minute before he came up with an envelope. It was folded and grimy, but Deglin smoothed it out and wrote across its face. He looked at the storage receipt for a moment, his jaw muscle working. His name was all in capital letters, except for the "e" in Deglin. That was a small letter. Then the date. And finally the signature, heavily penciled, "R. E. March." He put the receipt in the envelope and licked the flap and stuck it down firmly.

"There's a Captain Knight at Fifty-fourth Street. Acting Captain," he said.

"Heard of him."

"Give him this when you go off duty. Tell him Deglin gave it to you and that I'll be late."

The bartender took the envelope.

"And I'll have a drink," Deglin said.

He nursed the drink a little, sipping it, tasting it. He did that until he was tapped on the shoulder. Then he turned his head.

"You and me together," Smith said. "Brother, how I need it."

Smith's lank body was against the bar, and he leaned forward slightly to beckon the bartender. The bartender came over slowly. He turned his body, his hand at the bottles back of the bar, his expression questioning.

"That one there. No, there," Smith directed.

The bartender took the bottle and uncorked it. He got a glass and wiped it and set it in front of Smith. After he had poured the drink, he lifted his eyebrows at Deglin and Deglin nodded. The level of the glass raised itself with oily smoothness.

Smith waited until the bartender was down at the end of the bar again before he spoke.

"I saw you go out, Mark," he said. "I wish I'd gone with you."

Deglin said nothing.

"They're holding her," Smith said. "She'll break higher than a kite. She's scared to death right now."

"That's the way it goes," Deglin said. He let the whisky roll down his throat and signaled. "It was an accident. When you hang 'em, remember that, kid."

Smith shook his head. "Yeah, but I can't understand it. The thing that gets me is this. He wouldn't have run out, and neither would she. She wasn't going to run out on Paine alive. If you believe her, she walked in the goddamn rain all night deciding whether to run out on him. She wouldn't have run out on him dead. She and Redfield would have known they were in an awful jam but—" he looked at Deglin seriously, "people are people and they don't change much."

He watched Deglin put some money out on the bar and it occurred to him that he owed some money, too. He dug out some loose bills and dropped them beside Deglin's.

Deglin pushed his bills back as the bartender came over. They waited while the bartender brought back the change and laid it down. Deglin took it and shoved it in his pocket, and then, nodding, went on out.

Smith watched him go. He finished his drink and pushed it across the bar.

"Rough man," he said to the bartender, nodding at the door.

"I had a mind to whack him a while ago," the bartender confided.

Smith laughed.

18

Deglin took a cab to his apartment. He was no longer nervous or sick. Instead, there was an urgency in him, a driving need to move and move quickly. He could understand what he had done no more than he'd been able to understand other things that had happened to him his whole life long—moods that had swayed him, passions that had driven him.

The rain had settled in steadily, whipped and driven by the wind, and with it had come the early dusk. Lights gleamed sharply from the streets, wavering suddenly under new gusts. The figures of people hurried through the downpour.

He paid the driver off and hurried to the automatic elevator. It moved slowly up with him while his thoughts raced minutes ahead of himself. He'd need money—all he had—and his gun. And what else?

The elevator came soundlessly to a stop and the door opened. He came out, fumbling for his keys. He finally opened the door, and the lights of the living room glowed warmly.

He went in more slowly, his body slack, his urgency for the moment dissipated.

"Hello, Janie," he said.

She came out of the chair, smiling until she saw his face. Then she came to him at once and touched his cheek.

"Mark," she said.

"It's happened, Janie," he said. "I'm getting out."

She stepped back. For an instant her eyes searched his, her face lifted.

"I'll go with you, Mark," she said.

He shook his head, and for a moment it looked as though he was going to take her in his arms. He didn't. He stood, his body still loose.

"No, Jane," he said.

He walked past her to the bedroom and she followed. She watched him examine the small bedroom closet and take from it a heavier raincoat. He changed coats and went through the drawers of his dresser, finding some money and stuffing it in his pocket. Then he started to put cartridges in his pocket, thought of it momentarily, and took the cartridges out of his pocket again and put his gun beside them on the dresser.

That quickly he was ready.

"Will I see you, Mark?" she said, watching, wanting to help and not knowing how to.

"Maybe," he said. "Have you any money?"

It was something for her to do and she did it eagerly. She went to her pocketbook and took money from a billfold and handed it to him. "I can get more for you, Mark," she said.

"This is all right, Janie," he said.

He looked at her and for a moment the smile was in his eyes. Then it left and he said, "Look, baby, if anyone asks you, you haven't seen me. You haven't seen me, except for a couple of minutes at the Flamingo, for weeks. It'll be bad enough, as it is."

Then he went out the door and slammed it behind him.

He went hurriedly through the rain and the darkness to the corner. And there he stopped. A car went by slowly, its wheels splashing the puddles in bright arcs.

For a moment, as he stood in indecision, the picture came to him. It would not take long to get to the warehouse, not for Dan Riley. There would be Knight. It wouldn't take him long to plan this, to evaluate it, to put the dates together and consider their meanings. There would be Jeffries, smooth and enthusiastic . . . and the fingers on the teletype . . . and the voice on the radio . . . and slowly, like some waking giant, the whole vast resources of the department.

As the dog waits for the cat, and the cat waits for the mouse—

Run, Deglin.

RUN!

THE END

FILM NOIR CLASSICS

THE PITFALL Jay Dratler
"Dratler's novel is darker, sleazier and less forgiving than the film it inspired. A brutal portrait of blind lust and self-destruction..."—Cullen Gallagher, *Pulp Serenade*. Filmed in 1948 with Dick Powell, Lizbeth Scott, Jane Wyatt and Raymond Burr.

FALLEN ANGEL Marty Holland
"This story, about a small-time grifter who lands in a central California town and hooks up with a femme fatale, is straight out of the James M. Cain playbook."—Bill Ott, *Booklist*. Filmed in 1945 with Dana Andrews, Alice Faye and Linda Darnell.

THE VELVET FLEECE
Lois Eby & John C. Fleming
"We guarantee your head will be spinning with double-crosses and you'll be talking out of both sides of your mouth before you finish...." —*Evening Star*.
Filmed as *Larceny* in 1948 starring John Payne, Joan Caulfield and Dan Duryea.

SUDDEN FEAR Edna Sherry
"This is a thoroughly exciting read, with brilliant pacing, which makes you absolutely desperate to know how everything will pan out."—Kate Jackson. Filmed in 1952 with Joan Crawford, Jack Palance and Gloria Grahame.

HOLLOW TRIUMPH Murray Forbes
"...a disturbed personality done in the noir tradition... an atmospheric and evocative yarn that spans the late 30s to through WWII."—Amazon reader. Filmed in 1948 with Paul Henreid and Joan Bennett as *The Scar*.

THE DARK CORNER /
SLEEP, MY LOVE Leo Rosten
"The slang is tangy, the plots magnetic, the suspense sweet, the hilarity edgy... For all lovers of vintage noir."
—Donna Seaman, *Booklist*. Filmed in 1946 and 1948 with Lucille Ball, Clifton Well, Claudette Colbert and Robert Cummings.

DEADLIER THAN THE MALE
James Gunn
"The attitude of the book... reels between black comedy and surrealism drenched in a misanthropy that is occasionally stunning."—Ed Gorman. Filmed as *Born to Kill* in 1947 with Lawrence Tierney and Claire Trevor.

KISS THE BLOOD OFF MY HANDS
Gerald Butler
"The violence, crime, brutality, and 'trapped-in-a-narrow-place' aspects of noir are all here."—Carl Waluconis. Filmed in 1948 with Joan Fontaine and Burt Lancaster.

MOONRISE Theodore Strauss
"Moonrise is unique in that it's one of the few noirs in which the redemptive power of love holds nihilism at bay."—Eddie Muller. Filmed in 1948 with Dane Clark and Gail Russell.

Mad With Much Heart — Gerald Butler
"This is a page turner in the true sense of the word, starting with a car chase and culminating with a hazardous race up the side of a snow-covered hill."—Ron Koltnow. Filmed in 1951 by Nicholas Ray as *On Dangerous Ground* with Robert Ryan and Ida Lupino.

In trade paperback from...
Stark House Press, 1315 H Street, Eureka, CA 95501
greg@starkhousepress.com / www.StarkHousePress.com
Available from your local bookstore, or order direct via our website.